THE
OTHER SIDE
OF A
MURDER

S.J. BOYCE

S.J. BOYCE

Printed in the United States of America
First Printing 2021
First Edition 2021

ISBN: 979-8471002128

10 9 8 7 6 5 4 3 2 1

Cover Design by Rose Miller

Edited by Dana Micheli

DEDICATION

To my parents, for always being supportive of me, even during my questionable adventures. I love you both.

To my family and friends, thank you for believing in me and encouraging me throughout this journey. Your support means more than you will ever know.

A very special thank-you to, Karen Townsend, Michelle Turner and Jamie Dunlap for reading drafts of my novel and giving me wonderful feedback. Your help was so pivotal in making this project happen. I am sincerely thankful for your time and guidance. Love you lots.

To the ladies of NUBC, your support of this project pushed me to my limits. Thank you for getting me out of my comfort zone and expanding my reading list. Our Bookclub has developed into true friendship and I am very grateful for each one of you. Much love.

And to God most of all, because without God none of this would be possible.

PROLOGUE

TANYA L. JAMESON

J*ust my luck*, I thought as I glanced at my phone again, wondering how much longer we would be sitting on the tarmac. Actually, this had nothing to do with luck but my decision to fly out the day of the conference, rather than listening to my assistant. Ginger had suggested I arrive the day before, and as usual she was right. I had gotten to the airport on time and we boarded on time, only to be delayed – God only knew why – for an hour and counting.

Just then the pilot came over the intercom and announced we were ready for takeoff. As the engines came to life I turned off the phone and placed it in my bag. *Everything happens for a reason.* It was my go-to line whenever something didn't go right, and though I rarely knew what the reason was I was sticking to it, even when I spilled a cup of lousy plane coffee down the front of my blouse.

After a bumpy two-hour flight the plane touched down at Charlotte Douglas International Airport and I began the mad dash to collect my luggage and grab a taxi to the hotel. Since there was no time for check-in, I left my luggage with the concierge at the front desk and walked quickly toward the conference room, where the presentation on the future of diversity in accounting was already underway. I glanced around the packed room for an empty seat, and my gaze stopped on a very attractive brother with dark chocolate skin and striking features. I couldn't take my eyes off of him, and I thanked God I'd braved the turbulence to change my blouse in the airplane bathroom. It was blush pink and often got me several compliments, as did the shade of lipstick I had reapplied in the taxi.

I continued to scan the conference room for a seat. A blonde woman with a bright smile looked at me then pointed to an empty seat by her. As I started to approach her table, a woman sitting at the same as the attractive man gathered her belongings, got up and headed towards the exit doors. I looked from one table to the other and decided there was no way I was passing this opportunity up. I waved a thank you to the blonde woman and made my way to the man's table. He smiled at me as I took the now empty seat across from him. He looked familiar and for a second I wondered if we had met before. No way, I decided; his face was definitely not one I would forget.

Instead of listening to the presentation, I found myself studying this man – the way he laughed when the speaker said something amusing, the broadness of his shoulders, the meticulous grey suit and expensive cufflinks. *Who is this brother?* After thirty-seven years of living, it was the first time I'd had this level of instant attraction to someone.

Just then the speaker announced he was experiencing technical difficulties. As he fumbled with his PowerPoint, I sat there silently willing the handsome man to talk to me. Instead, the older white man with a thick, overgrown mustache on my left asked what company I worked for. With reluctance, I dragged my gaze toward him and replied that I was the VP of Finance at Brookes Brothers, a law firm in Saint Louis. I already knew what he would ask next: what our quarterly numbers were. The only reason some people attended these conferences was to see how they measured up to the competition, and I always gave them numbers much higher than what they actually were; I liked to see them sweat. As I politely rattled off the random figures, I felt the eyes of the handsome man on me. I glanced at him, feeling the heat rushing to my face as our eyes met, then quickly looked away.

After a few minutes the presentation resumed but I could barely follow it. When it finally ended, I glanced in the man's direction to find him gone. All around me people had started to get up from their seats and gather in circles to talk. With a sigh I pulled out my phone to check my email and suddenly felt someone's presence close by. I glanced up and right into the eyes of the handsome man.

"Your sales for this week must have been great," he said as he took the chair next to mine.

"Well, we *have* had the top sales for the past five years," I boasted.

He smiled, "Well not this year Ms….? " He paused, waiting for me to fill in the blank.

"Jameson," I said, blushing again, then fumbled in my bag for a business card.

"Ms. Jameson, I noticed that you came in late. Let's meet for dinner so I can brief you on what you missed."

I stared into his dark brown eyes. "I would like that."

"There's an excellent restaurant here in the hotel and the chef is a great friend of mine. Let's meet in the lobby at seven p.m." He stood and extended his hand. "By the way, I'm Jonathan Skagel, Financial Director at Brookes Brother, Chicago branch." He glanced down at the card. "Nice to finally meet you in person, Ms. Tan-ya L. Ja-me-son," he said, enunciating every syllable.

"Nice to meet you too, Mr. Skagel," I said, slightly embarrassed. As Financial Director he received the weekly emails I sent to the Directors. He also knew how much I had inflated the profits to the man with the mustache.

I was also annoyed with myself that I had never accompanied my boss on his quarterly trips to meet with the Directors of the other branches. It had always seemed like such a waste of time; now all I could think of was that I could have met the charming Mr. Skagel sooner.

"Looking forward to getting to know you better," he said, then excused himself to join some colleagues. I too noticed several people I should catch up with but quickly decided against it. I didn't know if it was the frustrating flight, the boring conference or nervousness about my dinner plans, but suddenly I was exhausted. With a friendly wave to a few familiar faces, I slipped from the room and headed to the front desk to check in. The hotel room was lovely, and after a long hot shower I set the alarm for six and slipped into bed.

For dinner with Jonathan, I wore a short black dress that accentuated my long legs. I pulled my micro braids into a bun and sprayed on my favorite cologne. I didn't know whether this dinner was personal, professional, or something in between, but I was going to be ready for it. I told myself it didn't matter – I would just focus on having a pleasant dinner. Yeah, right.

By six forty-five I was in the lobby and decided to wait at the bar so I wouldn't look too eager. The bar area was packed with men and women in business attire, most of whom I recognized from the conference. As I walked to an empty seat I noticed several men glancing in my direction, and one, a tall slender white man, tipped his glass towards me and gave a wide smile. I gave a gentle smile back and proceeded past him. These conferences were also known for hookups. I had engaged in several in the past, but not this time. I wanted something genuine.

I slid into a seat and ordered a glass of Merlot. As the bartender handed me my wine glass, I felt a light tap on my shoulder.

"May I join you?" I turned to see the smiling white guy. He wasn't bad-looking and in the past I may have taken him up on his offer, but not tonight.

"Well I am actually meeting –" I stopped at the touch of someone gently squeezing my shoulders. Even before I turned around I knew it was Jonathan. He gave a nod to the white man and grabbed my hand. "Our table is ready."

Feeling my heart quicken, I picked up the glass of Merlot with my free hand and allowed him to lead me to the table.

"Wow, you look great," Jonathan said, flashing that smile as he pulled out my chair. "I guess black is your color." He then went around to his side. That's when I noticed the two-piece black suit he was wearing. Though he looked damn good in it, he had clearly dressed for a business meeting. I slowly exhaled, knowing that this dinner was more professional than personal.

A part of me was disappointed because it had been a while since I enjoyed an intimate dinner with an intelligent man, especially one in the same field as me, but I decided to put my feelings aside and just enjoy the evening.

"You really look amazing", Jonathan stated again.

My heart began to beat fast. "Thank you." *Damn, this man has the charisma of Barack Obama.* I couldn't believe the feelings that were developing for him in such a short period of time. My grandma would always say, "Your heart will tell you when you meet the one." My heart, as well as other parts of me, was saying things, but I didn't know which one to trust.

As I skimmed the menu, Jonathan touched my hand and squeezed it.

"I have been here several times, so if I may I would like to order for us. I promise you won't be disappointed."

I took a sip of wine and nodded. The waiter greeted us and poured water into our empty glasses. Without looking at the menu, Jonathan placed our order. The waiter jotted it down without question then gave a half-bow and walked away. I raised an eyebrow at Jonathan.

He took a sip of his water and smiled. "What is that look for?"

"Half of what you ordered isn't even on the menu."

"I told you the chef is a personal friend."

"I see. Well, my palate is fully in your hands." I said, raising the wine glass to my lips again.

Jonathan leaned in closer and I could smell his enticing cologne. "I promise you won't regret it," he whispered.

I took another sip of wine to control the wide grin that started to form on my face. Before the appetizers arrived, Jonathan told me everything I missed in the meeting, which wasn't much.

Good, I thought, *get the boring stuff out of the way so we can spend the rest of the night getting acquainted.*

The waiter placed a platter of bacon-wrapped duck between us. I sighed as I sunk my teeth into it.

"Wow," I mumbled.

Jonathan smiled. "I hope you brought your appetite because this is only the beginning."

I nodded vigorously as I popped the other half of the duck in my mouth. We both burst into laughter.

For the main entrées Jonathan had ordered the pan-seared jumbo scallops with citrus risotto, butter garlic herb cream with truffle oil and red snapper with quinoa and Swiss chard. Jonathan insisted that I try everything, so he had the waiter bring us extra plates and he fixed one for me, putting a little of everything on it. I was in heaven, my body tingling every time I put something new in my mouth. I had never tasted food this good before.

Jonathan's eyes were on me with every new bite, a smile forming on his face as I closed my eyes to enjoy the flavors that were dancing on my taste buds. Over dinner, I learned that Jonathan had been working for Brookes Brothers for the past eight years. He is the oldest of four children, he had a brother, Michael, in his third year of residency at Meharry Medical College in Nashville, and a sister, Karen, who taught third grade in Bowie, Maryland. His youngest brother, Alan, was in grad school at Hampton University. I told him that I was the only child and a native of Georgia, where my parents still lived. Then the conversation turned to dating, with both of us telling some of our best and worst experiences.

He'd certainly had his share of both, and in between laughs I told him I hadn't realized how hard it was for men to date as well.

We were enjoying each other so much that we lost track of time. Suddenly Jonathan winked at me and said, "I think we should leave." I glanced around the restaurant and realized we were the only patrons left; our waiter stood a few feet away, staring as if willing us to leave. I nodded in agreement and he signaled for the check.

A few minutes later we were heading to the elevators, Jonathan's hand never leaving the small of my back. We were on the same floor, and we made our way down the long hallway to my room, I sensed that he wanted me to invite him in. To be honest, parts of me wanted that too, but I wanted this to be more than just sex. I wanted a real relationship and I saw that potential in Jonathan. We said our goodbyes at the door.

After removing my makeup and preparing for bed, I was surprised when the room phone rang. I had a feeling before I answered that it was him.

"Hi, Tanya, I was just calling to make sure you were settled in okay."

Since he just walked me to my room, I thought it was weird, but I went with it.

"Yes, I am settled in," I blushed, then sat on my bed.

"I had a really good time tonight Tanya."

"So did I."

"I know we live in different states, but I am in Saint Louis often for meetings and I would really love to see you again, if that's okay with you."

"Yes, I would like that."

"I look forward to getting to know you better Ms. Ja-me-son, have a wonderful night."

"You too Mr. Skagel." A wide smile formed on my face and I put the receiver down. I was blushing like a schoolgirl. I laid in the bed and pulled the covers over my body, then closed my eyes.

CHAPTER 1

TANYA L. JAMESON

I walked out of the elevator onto the second floor of Brookes Brothers Law Firm feeling refreshed. My hips swayed in my navy knee-length fitted skirt that hugged me just right. I wore a cream-colored blouse and my favorite five-inch red Jimmy Choo pumps. I walked into the office feeling like Naomi Campbell on the runway. I knew I looked good.

The past two months with Jonathan had been amazing, despite the distance between us. Jonathan knew the best restaurants both in Chicago and Saint Louis and loved taking me to them. And he was so chivalrous, always holding the door open for me and bringing me flowers or jewelry every time he saw me. We enjoyed every moment we spent together, had even started talking about what our future might look like, kids and all.

Last night was one of the best nights that we'd have ever had. We both loved to travel and we were planning a trip to Paris in a few months. Jonathan became excited as he described his trip to Paris last summer – how the food was exquisite and how he couldn't wait to experience it with me. I'd laughed when he asked me to sit on his lap, but after several minutes with my head on his chest, listening to his heart beat, I felt calm and relaxed. Then, instead of making love like we usually did, Jonathan held me in his arms and rocked me to sleep. I woke up the next morning rested and wanting him more than I ever wanted him before.

I glanced up at Jonathan to see him in a peaceful sleep. I removed his hands from my waist and straddled him, then placed small kisses over his face and neck. His body shifted as he let out a quiet moan, then I felt the rise of him pressing against me. I moved my thong to the side and enveloped him, moving rhythmically as his hands gripped my ass. What I was feeling at this moment was so intense I couldn't control my body. I'd never felt like this before with anyone. Jonathan whispered my name in my ear as his breathing became faster and faster.

"I love you," he whispered.

With the sound of those words, I collapsed on him and screamed out his name in total ecstasy.

After making love to Jonathan for the second time, I heard the alarm of my phone dinging. It was my weekly reminder for the eight a.m. Monday meeting that I held. It was 7:37.

"Damn it!" I said out loud.

Jonathan sat up. "Is everything okay?"

"I just have to make a phone call." I called Ginger and told her to cancel the meeting because I wasn't feeling well. I told her that I would be in later on and if she needed my immediate attention to call or email me. When I hung up Jonathan was already out of bed and getting ready to go to the airport. It was getting harder and harder each time we separated.

"I'll drive you," I said sadly.

"Nope, I'm taking a taxi. I don't want you to be any later to work."

He was very considerate like that.

Two hours later, I walked into my corner office; Ginger immediately followed.

"Good morning, Tanya, how are you feeling?"

"Hi Ginger, better, thanks," I said, feeling a little guilty about that lie.

"Good. Mr. Brookes would like to see you in his office."

Ginger Spence, a petite redheaded twenty-seven-year-old, had been with me for three years. She was a good assistant; I would even consider her a close friend.

"Was Charles upset when I canceled the meeting?"

"It's hard to say, he has been in a weird mood this morning. Good luck." Ginger gave me a halfhearted smile as she exited my office.

Mr. Charles Brookes, Jr., was the nicest boss I'd ever had and, like Ginger, had also become a close personal friend. A biracial man in his late thirties, Charles stood six-foot-two with broad shoulders, curly hair and an infectious smile. The ladies loved him, and though he was *too pretty* for me – jocks were more my speed – I understood why. He took great pride in his appearance, and most mornings could be found working out in the gym on the top floor of the building. Sometimes he even went back after work.

Charles's father, Charles Brookes, Sr., was one of the founding members of Brookes Brothers, along with his brothers, Adam and Leland Brookes. Charles and his father worked out of the Missouri branch and oversaw all the financial operations, the uncles, were stationed in West Virginia.

Brookes Brothers was founded in the late 1980s after Charles Sr. was abruptly fired from the law firm where he worked. The official reason was that the firm was downsizing, but Charles knew it was really based on his decision to marry a black woman. After unsuccessfully trying to find a job at another local law, and learning that his new bride was pregnant, Charles Sr. decided to start his own company. His motto was "Family First," and he ensured that the company policies supported this. When his brothers, Adam, an accountant, and Leland, a criminal law attorney, partnered with him, the company soared. It was now one of the biggest law firms in the world, handling everything from mergers and acquisitions to pro bono cases for those who could not afford their exorbitant rates.

I had interned at Brookes Brothers the summer of 2004, my senior year of college, and loved every minute of it. I knew this was where I wanted to build my career. After I graduated with my accounting degree, they offered me an entry-level position which I eagerly accepted. I eventually went back to get another bachelor's degree, this one specializing in tax law. After several years of handling tax cases, I found that I really enjoyed the accounting side of the job and that I was really good at it. Charles Jr. and Sr. both agreed and after several years of hard work, I was promoted to VP of Finance. Throughout my fifteen years at Brooke Brothers, Charles Jr. had gone out of his way to acknowledge my department and my work. He had also become the big brother I never had. We rarely went a day without speaking and we had lunch a couple of times a week.

Unfortunately, being friends with the boss had its downside. Charles and I had been spending so much time together that rumors started circulating about our relationship. None of them were true, but the way Charles would look at me and openly compliment my appearance and intelligence had tongues wagging and I wasn't about to go there. I wanted people to know I'd earned my advancement on my own merit, not because I was involved with the founder's son. Since then, I had pulled back a bit, though I still deeply valued our friendship.

As I walked to his fifth-floor office, I wondered whether Charles was upset about this morning's meeting or if something else was going on. Renee, his assistant, told me to go right in. I gently knocked and then opened the door.

"You wanted to see me, Mr. Brookes...?" I said formally as I poked my head in.

"Yes, please...come in and have a seat, Tanya." Charles pointed to the chair across from his desk. He then rose from his chair and began walking around his desk.

I looked at him. "I'm sorry about having to reschedule the meeting this morning on such short notice."

He sat in the chair next to the one I was sitting in. "That's okay, Ginger told me that you weren't feeling well this morning. Actually, I was surprised when Joe told me he'd seen you in the parking garage."

Joe - now there's another character; the little snot-nosed prick had been trying to undercut me for the last two years.

"How are you feeling now, Tanya?" Charles asked, his tone sincere.

"I'm feeling okay now," I said, touching my stomach. "You know, women issues."

Charles paused for a beat, looking uncomfortable. "I wanted to ask you something…" he got up from the chair and walked over to the door. "It's a personal request." He closed the door and walked back to the chair and sat down.

"You're scaring me," I said, my body shifting in the chair.

"Oh, it's nothing that serious. I'm getting my condo remodeled and I need somewhere to stay for two or three weeks and I was just wondering…" A slight grin formed on Charles's face as he lingered on the word wondering.

"Are you asking to stay with me?" I stood and shot him an incredulous look. "Charles, you know the gossip about us has just died down, and this is just going to open the whole thing up again."

"Tanya, you know I don't care about rumors. This is my dad's company, I am the boss and folks will always have something to say. The same goes for you, given your position." Charles stood and walked closer to me. "You know I hate hotels and my friends don't have the room. To be honest I wouldn't want to stay with them anyway. So what do you say, roomie...? I make a mean margarita." He bumped his shoulder to my shoulder.

I laughed. "You're crazy, but I guess that'll be okay."

Charles smiled and extended his hand in a professional gesture. "Thanks, Tanya, I really appreciate it." I shook his hand and walked out of his office.

It wasn't until I was back at my own desk when I realized I'd forgotten all about Jonathan. We had decided to keep our relationship a secret and since we didn't work directly with each other it had been easy thus far. We just made sure not to use company email or phone to discuss our personal relationship. Even though there wasn't a company policy prohibiting in-house relationships I had seen enough of them over the years to know the woman never came out on top.

I left work early to tidy my place, making sure the smell of Jonathan's enticing cologne was out of the air. I also made sure that no bras or panties were hanging in the spare bedroom. That room had many functions: my yoga studio, my clothes drying rack, and my "deal with it later" pile. I dusted, vacuumed, and put fresh linen on the bed so it was ready for my new roommate.

Since I was already preparing dinner for myself, I made a little extra just in case Charles was hungry. The doorbell rang just as I was finishing. I glanced at the clock: 7:07 p.m. I tasted the sauce, then put my spoon down and turned off the eyes on the stove before going to open the door. Charles stood with three suitcases with a cheery smile on his face.

"Wow, you have a lot of stuff, are you sure it's only going to be for two weeks?" I questioned as I stepped aside to allow Charles to enter.

"I said two or three weeks, and you women aren't the only ones who like options," Charles smirked as he brought the suitcases in the house and lined them by the front door. He stopped and glanced around my place. This was only the second time he had been here; the first was when he accompanied me to look at it when I was thinking about buying.

"Wow, it hardly looks like the same place," Charles stated as he walked over to the painting that hung in my living space. "And this is amazing!"

I smiled at the compliment. I was particularly proud of the piece he was admiring – a naked silhouette of a voluptuous woman lying on a beach with the sun shining down on her. It was raw, sexy and enchanting all at the same time, and it captivated everyone who saw it.

"Thanks, I bought it at a gallery opening last summer. The brother was an up-and-coming artist, so I got this for a steal. You should see how much his paintings are going for now!" I walked over and stood by Charles, taking it in. With its bright colors and a hint of turquoise that covered the sky, it matched my décor to a tee.

Suddenly he sniffed the air and rubbed his stomach. "What smells so good?"

"Are you hungry?" I smiled and walked towards the kitchen. "I made shrimp pasta with garlic bread."

"I didn't know you cook," he said as he went to the sink and washed his hands.

"Well, there are a lot of things that you don't know about me." I brought the main dish with the basket of bread to the table, then pointed to the counter. "Grab that bottle of wine."

Charles looked in the direction I pointed in, then collected the wine and the opener and took them to the table. As I plated our food, he opened the wine and poured each of us a generous glass.

Charles twirled some pasta around his fork and placed it in his mouth. "This is delicious!"

"Thank you." I took a sip of wine.

"Tanya, I'm really grateful that you're allowing me to crash here, and trust me, I won't say anything about this at the office. I know how you don't want people in our business."

"Okay…" I said, relieved. "You may not know this being the owner's son and all, but a lot of people didn't think that I deserved that promotion and they haven't been silent about making that known."

"Oh, I know more than you think. That's why I'm saying we keep this just between us. That includes Ginger."

This struck me as a little odd, as he knew I trusted her implicitly. "You got something against Ginger?" I smirked.

Charles shrugged. "As I said, I know more than you think." He looked at his wine glass. "Do you have anything stronger?"

I pointed to the cabinet above my refrigerator, then continued eating in silence while Charles grabbed the bourbon and poured himself a hefty glass. I didn't know what to think about his comment about Ginger, but I made a mental note to be more careful around her.

Charles and I spent the rest of the evening talking about our family, friends and hobbies. Something he stated while sipping on his third glass of bourbon made me a little cautious. We were talking about college and how much fun it was being that young and carefree. Charles mentioned how much he wanted to be a doctor, something he'd never talked about before. When I asked him why he decided to join his dad's company instead of pursuing a career in medicine, he went silent, then quietly stated, "No medical school would admit me with my record."

"Record? What do you mean?" I questioned.

Charles quietly got up from the couch and walked into the kitchen, where he placed his empty bourbon glass on the counter before heading down the short hallway. I said nothing, just watched in silence as he entered the guest room, closed the door and locked it behind him. I leaned back on the couch and poured myself another glass of wine.

Well, this is going to be an interesting three weeks.

CHAPTER 2

TANYA L. JAMESON

Having Charles stay with me had its benefits. He'd gotten into the habit of making breakfast in the mornings and his banana pancakes was totally worth getting up early for. I had also gotten into work on time each day, sometimes even early. On the other hand, I was freaking out that people would discover our arrangement, and by "people" I mostly meant Jonathan. I had called him several times, only to have his phone go straight to voicemail. I knew how easily things are found out in an office setting, and though Charles and I had been very careful, I was worried that Jonathan had heard something.

It didn't help matters that Jonathan didn't care much for Charles – he had made that clear during our past conversations about work. He thought Charles was a micromanager and spoiled. I never acknowledged these comments, because I didn't want to badmouth my friend and I didn't want Jonathan to know how close Charles and I were.

I was careful with Charles as well; we talked about past relationships but I never hinted that I was currently dating someone, and certainly not someone at Brookes Brothers. Then again, the way things were going I didn't even know if I was still dating Jonathan.

Just when I was beginning to think he was a figment of my imagination, he "replied to all" to an email that Charles had sent to the team about the upcoming quarterly reports.

I stared at the curt response: My team is on track with meeting this deadline, JFS. "So, he is alive," I mumbled. The last two weeks of radio silence had me doubting his feelings for me. They certainly felt serious when we were together, so what had happened?

It was Friday and I was in my office rereading a report for the third time. Finally I laid it down on my desk and exhaled. My mind wasn't there; it was on Jonathan. The eerie silence in the building made me suddenly aware of the time: 6:32 p.m. Normally the hallways would still be abuzz with top executives and assistants rushing from one meeting to another, but today they had left at 4:30 to get ready for the Saint Louis Branch's Annual Banquet. Everyone in the office looked forward to this event every year. The firm spared no expense; the location was usually very nice, and the food and music were always exceptional. The women wore evening gowns and the men wore tuxes. It was fun to see everyone so relaxed and free, rather than their usual stressed-out selves. This year, however, I just wasn't feeling it.

Maybe it was because I was thinking about Jonathan and hoped he was okay. It has been a full two-weeks since I had heard from him. I didn't know whether to be angry or worried.

Just then the phone rang, and I prayed for the hundredth time that it might be him. Instead, I heard Charles's voice on the other end.

"Tell me why you're still at work, I thought you said you were leaving an hour ago."

I sighed with disappointment. "I don't feel like being very social tonight. I have a couple of reports that need wrapping up then I just want to go home, order Chinese food and watch Netflix. Besides, I don't have a date again this year and I really don't want to spend another sad evening in the corner by myself, watching all the couples dance."

"Well you'd better get your memory checked, because from what I recall you refused to dance with half the guys who asked you, including me." Charles chuckled. "As your boss and good friend I am demanding you to leave work and come to the banquet or I'll be forced to abandon ship and join you on the couch. You know that if neither of us shows up you can expect major stares on Monday."

"Well, I definitely wouldn't want that," I said. The phone went silent and I hoped I hadn't hurt his feelings. "Okay, I'll go, but you should go ahead because I'll probably be arriving late."

"Okay, I'll see you there," he stated with slightly less enthusiasm.

~ ~ ~

The firm had really outdone itself this year. The affair was held at the Four Seasons, the finest hotel in Saint Louis. The floors of the grand ballroom were marbled, with thick curtains draped to the floor from the ceiling. Normally I would have taken a moment to appreciate it, but that night all I saw were the couples gliding on the dance floor as the band played Earth, Wind & Fire's "Dancing in September."

Ginger spotted me and walked over to introduce me to her date for the evening; I could never keep up with Ginger's men.

"I thought you weren't coming," she said, eyeing the red strapless dress that looked damn good on me, if I said so myself.

"Well, someone changed my mind," I replied.

Ginger gave me a curious look. "Oh, really?"

I ignored her and glanced pointedly at her date, a guy who was about five-foot-eight and stocky; just her type.

"I would like you to meet Thomas."

Thomas reached out his hand and I shook it. Then Ginger slipped her arm through his and looked at me. "Come sit with us, we have an extra seat at our table."

I was hoping to sit with Charles but thought that would look suspicious so I said okay and followed them to table five. Already seated there was Mr. Willis and his wife, Ingrid. Mr. Willis was an elderly white gentleman who had been with Brookes Brothers for twenty-two years. Sitting beside Ingrid, was Margaret, the Director of Human Resources, and her husband, Mike. Then there was me, the only one without a date. For the next thirty minutes I politely listened to the Willises talk about their children, grandchildren and great-grandchildren but when they pulled out photos, I decided enough was enough. It was time for a drink. I politely excused myself and headed to the bar.

Walking to the bar, I saw Charles talking to his dad by the door. Charles spotted me and started to walk my way but was sidetracked by Terry, the newest receptionist. She had secured the position two weeks earlier thanks to her father, who was the Director of Marketing, and since then had proven herself to be inefficient and a gossiper. She had also made it very obvious that she wanted Charles.

Charles pleaded with me with his eyes to come save him, but I just smiled, turned to the bar, and ordered a drink. Ten minutes later, Charles finally saw his chance to escape when an intern walked by. He introduced the two, then quickly headed for the bar.

"Thanks a lot," he said as he walked up beside me.

I grinned, sipping my gin and tonic as Charles sat on the empty stool next to mine. He motioned for the bartender, who poured a shot of tequila and placed it in front of him.

"My dad went all-out this year!" Charles said, looking around.

"He really did." I smiled. "I'm glad I came – thanks for convincing me." I eyed his glass. "You're already taking shots?"

Just then the band started to play Stevie Wonder's "Superstition." Charles gulped his tequila, then took the glass out of my hand and pulled me to the dance floor. I could feel eyes staring at us as we made our way to the center of the floor. Charles must have sensed my discomfort because he pulled me close to him and whispered, "Just relax and have fun." And I did just that; I ignored all the whispers and the stares and moved with his rhythm. I didn't have a care in the world, and just for the moment I felt free, relaxed and secure.

The music slowed and the crowd began to applaud as the CEO, Charles Brookes Sr. walked onto the stage. I noticed that I was still holding Charles' hand and quickly let go of it. He smiled, then moved to take the stage with his father. A cheer went up from the crowd when Mr. Brookes announced that our numbers were the highest out of all of the branches, which meant that everyone would be receiving a bonus.

"We would like to give special thanks to the VP of Finance, Tanya Jameson, and her team, for leading the way this quarter. They have implemented a new reporting system that will not only save us time while producing more accurate data but will also reduce costs. Ms. Jameson, would you please join us?"

All eyes were riveted on me as I approached the stage. Charles Sr. gently patted my arm and handed me an award. "You and your team will receive the Brookes Brothers award for this year!"

I stared down in amazement. The Brookes Brothers Award not only gave you bragging rights but came with a hefty bonus as well. Even as I thanked him, I couldn't help but notice the stares and whispers that came with the round of applause. I didn't care at this point, though, because I realized that Charles was right; no matter what you did or how hard you worked people still gossiped. There was nothing I could do but relish in the moment and proudly accept the award on behalf of my department.

For the rest of the night, people came up to me to offer their congratulations. Some of them seemed sincere, and I decided I was just being paranoid; not all of them were out for me. I looked around the room for Charles to thank him as well, but he had disappeared.

After an unsuccessful search for him I left the party and arrived at my house a little after eleven. When I walked in, I smelled the sweet aroma of my favorite candles, which were lit all around the room. Soft jazz played in the background and two glasses of champagne were on the table. The first thing that came to my mind was Jonathan, but that's not who came around the corner holding a dozen of red roses in his hand.

"Charles...!" I exclaimed.

He held up a finger and walked over to me, then handed me the roses. "This is just to show you how much I appreciate you dealing with me for the last couple of weeks, and to congratulate you on your award tonight – nothing more." He picked up two glasses of champagne from the counter.

I placed the roses down on the table and took one of the glasses out of his hand.

"What do you mean, nothing more?" I glanced around the room. "This looks like a lot more... a simple thank you and maybe a box of chocolates would've sufficed."

"Tanya, why do you have your guard up all the time? Can't anyone do something for you just because?"

"No, Charles, they can't, because it's never 'just because.'" I sighed. "Look... everything is so beautiful and I enjoy your company, but you don't have to go out of your way to do things for me, like in the meetings and then tonight–"

Charles interrupted me. "I had nothing to do with tonight, Tanya. Whether you believe it or not you are a valued asset to our company. Yes, I admit that I sometimes go out of my way to make sure everyone realizes how valuable you are, and I'm sorry if that makes you uncomfortable, but that award was all you."

"I'm sorry," I said, sighing again. "This is really sweet of you… thank you."

"So, can we relax now? I rented a movie for us."

"A movie, it's almost midnight!" I said and then caved. "Okay, let me go change into something a little more comfortable."

Charles gave me a mischievous look.

"Like sweats," I added, then walked up the stairs to my bedroom. We spent the rest of the night, drinking the champagne and talking, and I had so much fun I almost forgot about Jonathan ghosting me. Almost.

~   ~   ~

I woke the next morning to the sound of a ringing phone and the feeling of a jackhammer at my temple. It was the worst hangover I'd had since college. The phone rang twice then stopped abruptly. I didn't even care if Charles had answered; I was just glad it stopped ringing.

Moments later, Charles knocked on my door. "Yeah," I said in a light whisper.

"The telephone is for you," Charles said, so quietly I could barely hear him. He must've been feeling like I was.

"Okay, thanks," I said, reaching for the phone on the nightstand. Aside from my parents, I was the only person I knew who still had a landline. I considered it an unnecessary expense but indulged my overprotective father who felt better knowing I always had access to a phone. "Hello?"

"Tanya, are you okay?"

Jonathan!

I sat up in my bed, ignoring the wave of nausea, and pulled off my headscarf. *Stop it, Tanya,* I chided myself silently, *he can't see you.*

"Jonathan, is that you?"

"Who else would it be?" he said with a curt tone. There was a moment of silence. "I'm sorry Tanya, I guess I have been MIA lately, and that's why I am calling." There was another awkward silence, then he asked tentatively, "Do you have a houseguest? The voice sounds familiar."

"Huh?" For a moment I didn't know what he was talking about, then I remembered that Charles had answered my phone. "Oh, you mean the guy who answered my phone. He's a friend of mine who needed a place to crash for a couple weeks while his condo is being remodeled." Silence again. I was hoping that Jonathan wouldn't ask more detailed questions about who the person was because I didn't want to start lying to him. "Jonathan... I thought we had something special, but it doesn't seem like you feel the same way, so we can end this awkward conversation and just go our separate ways."

"No! Tanya, sweetie, of course I feel the same way. Its work – things aren't going well and I haven't been in a great mood. I didn't want to take it out on you so I thought it would be best to distant myself until I got my mind straight. If you let me, I would like to spend the rest of the weekend making it up to you." he paused. "Will you allow me to show you how sorry I am?"

"I suppose I will let you try," I replied hesitantly but I was already smiling. "What time do you get in?" He told me, then I said, "I don't want to stay here in town, can we go somewhere?"

I didn't want to think about his reaction if he ran into Charles at my place.

"Sure, I have access to a cottage."

"Sounds perfect, I'll pick you up at the airport and we can head straight there."

"Well, then I'll see you in a couple of hours." He paused. "Love you, sweetie."

I hung up the phone without saying I love you back; I wanted to look into his eyes to see if he really meant those words.

I took a shower, then started packing an overnight bag when Charles knocked at my door.

"Come in," I said pulling a cute summer dress from my closet.

Charles entered my room. "Are you okay? I was thinking that maybe we can go for lunch." He paused when he spotted the overnight bag on my bed. "Oh, I didn't know you were going anywhere."

"Well I wasn't, but a friend just called and I'll be going away for the weekend. Don't worry, I'll be back and on time for the Monday morning meeting." I chuckled.

"A friend, huh?" Charles watched me as I held up a negligee. My face reddened as I followed his gaze and I quickly stuffed it in my bag. "You haven't told me about this special friend, is this something serious or just a fling?"

"I don't do flings," I said as I zipped the bag and started to pick it up but Charles grabbed it and pointed to the door. I grabbed my purse and keys and walked out. "I'll take a raincheck on lunch," I said over my shoulder. Charles didn't say anything; he just followed me outside to my car.

An uncomfortable silence hung between us as we walked out to my car. I hit the unlock button on my key fob and slid into the driver's seat while he placed my overnight bag on the back seat.

"Thank you, Charles."

Charles closed the back door, then grabbed my door. "Have a good weekend Tanya," he said, gently closing it for me. I sat there for a minute, watching as he walked back into the house and closed the door. Suddenly, part of me wanted to go back in and spend the day with him. Charles always had something fun planned for us and I had enjoyed spending time with him these last couple of weeks. I wasn't sure what my feelings for him were, but in that moment I was actually torn between him and Jonathan.

"This better be worth it," I said to myself as turned on the engine and backed out my driveway.

~ ~ ~

The drive to the airport was hell, and not just because of the traffic. My mind was all over the place, switching between images of Jonathan's smile and Charles's broad shoulders as he handed me a glass of champagne. Charles and I were just friends, but I couldn't shake the feelings I was developing for him. It was only after a second narrowly avoided accident that I forced my attention to the road.

Finally, I pulled into the short-term parking lot at the airport. I looked at the clock and smiled – despite the traffic and stopping to pick up some Italian for dinner I still had plenty of time before Jonathan's flight arrived. I loved browsing the various shops and the boutiques in the terminal. After one of my recent trips, I'd stumbled onto a black-owned smoothie shop. The owner, Samantha, was an athletic-type sister with long boxed braids and a kind, genuine smile. She'd greeted me as I walked in and let me try several different smoothies before I settled on the Tropical Breeze, a mix of spinach, pineapple and berries. That day, we sat and chatted for an hour.

I walked quickly to the shop, hoping Samantha would be there. I wanted another one of those delicious smoothies. I also wanted an unbiased opinion about Jonathan and Charles. My mouth watered as I spotted the "*S is for Smoothie*" sign, I could see Samantha in the store assisting a customer and she had two more customers waiting. Instead of waiting in line, I decided to browse my favorite scarf store.

As I picked up a beautiful pink scarf, two arms grabbed me around my waist and twirled me around. I let out a scream of surprise and fright, then realized I was looking into the eyes of Jonathan.

"Oh my God, where did you come from?!" My heart racing, I leaned up and kissed him.

"My flight landed early so I decided to get you a gift." Jonathan held up a small gift box and smiled. I was happy to see him but disappointed that I wouldn't get a chance to talk to Samantha. He handed me the box, then grabbed my hand and his carry-on and guided me towards the exit doors.

As we passed the smoothie shop, Samantha happened to be looking out the window. I smiled warmly at her, but she looked back with a perplexed look on her face. Oh well; she probably met so many people there was no reason to think she'd remember our conversation that day.

All thoughts of Samantha and smoothies faded as Jonathan brought my hand to his lips and kissed it.

"I'm so excited to see you."

When we got to my car Jonathan gently took the keys out of my hand and opened the passenger door. I got in, then he leaned in and kissed me; this time it was a long lingering kiss and it felt good. He licked his lips and made a moaning sound as he moved his face back from mine, while I just stared into his eyes as if I would find my answers there. He closed my door, put his luggage in the trunk, and got in the driver's seat. I placed the little unopened box in my lap.

As he slid into the driver's seat he glanced at the box, then shot a questioning look at me. "Aren't you going to open it?"

"I'm not sure."

"Just open it," he said, removing his hands from the steering wheel. "I won't move until you do."

I stared at the box, not sure why I was hesitating. Jonathan turned off the ignition, took the box out of my hand, and opened his car door.

"What are you doing?"

He didn't answer, just walked around the car to my side then opened my door and reached in to unbuckle my seatbelt.

"What is this?" I asked.

"Well you must have great instincts; it is meant for me to open for you…" Jonathan got on one knee.

I gasped as he opened the box to reveal a diamond ring. It was a big one, too, at least two carats. I put my hand to my mouth. Jonathan grabbed my left hand and said those four little words that I'd been waiting to hear since I was a little girl.

"Will you marry me?"

"You didn't just buy this at the airport!" I exclaimed, looking at the ring.

"Tanya, really, I am here on bended knee," Jonathan laughed.

"Yes! Yes! Yes! I will marry you!" I said, then suddenly I was out of the car and in his arms.

I was still feeling dazed a few minutes later as we pulled onto the highway and headed toward the cottage. Every few minutes I would look down at my left hand, now intertwined with his, as if expecting it to be gone. It was almost as if I had imagined the whole thing.

Jonathan had told me the cottage was just sixty miles away, but the drive seemed to take much longer. Maybe it was because I was wondering what had just happened. Jonathan's proposal had been so out of the blue, especially since we hadn't spoken in weeks. I knew I loved him and wanted to be with him, but I couldn't help but wonder if I'd been right to accept his proposal so quickly.

Jonathan was unusually quiet for most of the drive, though he responded to my light conversation saying all the right things. He seemed genuinely happy when I told him about the company's banquet and my award, congratulating me and gently kissing my hand. Yet every now and then I could feel his eyes on me, it felt intense and awkward.

We arrived at the cottage around 5:15 that evening. After bringing our bags in, Jonathan went straight for the shower while I went to the kitchen to heat up dinner. A few minutes later he emerged, looking every bit as handsome in sweats and tee as he did in his suits. He smiled at the plates of pasta I'd set on the table, then grabbed a bottle of wine and a couple of glasses from the counter. Over dinner we caught each other up on the past few weeks, but neither of us mentioned our very recent engagement or future plans.

"Would you like to go for a walk?" I said, touching his arm. "It's a wonderful night outside."

"Maybe tomorrow, sweetie, I am really tired and just want to head to bed." Jonathan stood up from the table, then looked at me. "You coming?"

"I think I will clean up a bit. I will be up shortly." I watched Jonathan walk to the bedroom.

A few minutes later I stood overnight bag in hand, about to head upstairs. The dishes had been washed and put away and the countertops were sparkling, but my thoughts were still racing. I set the bag down and turned toward the door, deciding a walk along the lake was exactly what I needed to clear my head. I slipped outside and began at a leisurely pace past an array of lovely cottages. One had a large back deck and I noticed an elderly black couple sitting there, their hands intertwined like teenagers in love. I wondered if Jonathan and I would be this happy when we reached their age.

They saw me staring at them and waved me over. I smiled, my walk momentarily forgotten, and walked toward them.

"What cottage are you in, dear?" the woman asked, returning my smile.

I pointed to the light blue cottage across the water.

"Oh, that's the Spence's place," the woman said to her husband, who nodded.

I thought about my assistant, Ginger Spence, and how she always talked about her parents' cottage on the lake. Could this be it? If so, it was a strange coincidence.

"It's a nice place," the woman remarked, interrupted my thoughts.

"Yes, it is. My fiancé and I are here for the weekend." I smiled again as I said the word fiancé, though it felt strange.

"Oh, that's nice," the gentleman replied, "Where is he?"

"He had a long flight, he is resting," I said, embarrassed because Jonathan's flight was under two hours. They asked if I wanted to join them for a glass of wine and I happily accepted.

Two hours later we were still chatting away. I noticed the way they looked at each other and finished each other's sentences, and couldn't help but wonder if Jonathan and I would ever have this type of connection. Although I loved him, I knew we weren't at the point of marriage. I had gotten caught up in the moment and said yes without thinking it through. The fact that he didn't mention it at dinner made me think he had reservations as well.

After another glass of wine I bid the elderly couple goodnight and made my way back to the cottage. Jonathan was still sound asleep. Instead of waking him by using the shower in the master suite, I decided to shower in the downstairs bathroom and sleep on the couch. There was a lot to think about and my visit with the neighbors had left me even more confused about what to do about this marriage proposal.

The next morning I was awakened by soft kisses on my cheek.

"Hi sweetie, why did you sleep out here?" Jonathan spoke softly.

"I was restless and didn't want to wake you."

I sat up to make room on the sofa for him. He lowered himself onto it and wrapped his arms around me. I laid my head on his chest.

"I'm sorry for crashing so early last night. I was just so exhausted." He touched my left hand, rubbing the ring that he'd placed there less than twenty-four hours ago, then brought it up to his mouth and kissed it. "Today, I am all yours, anything you want to do, we will do."

"Well you could start by making me breakfast," I said.

"You got it. I just have to run to the store to pick up a few things." Jonathan kissed me on the cheek. "I'm going to make you something special."

"Sounds perfect."

I watched appreciatively as he stood and stretched. He was smart, FINE, and charming – everything I wanted in a man. Yet I couldn't' deny that there was something off about our relationship, that there was a distance between us. Was it Charles and the way I was now feeling about him? I didn't know what it was, but I had to figure it out before we said our "I do's."

CHAPTER 3

TANYA L. JAMESON

That Monday morning I woke with a gloomy feeling I just couldn't shake. We'd had a great time at the cabin, but it was unlike any other weekend I'd spent with Jonathan. Even after breakfast, which was fabulous, and after making love, something still felt off. My gut was trying to tell me something, but I didn't know exactly what. Was it my imagination that our goodbye at the airport was a bit awkward? Was it because we had still not discussed the proposal? I thought about it the whole drive home, but the answers continued to elude me.

I stopped home to shower and dress for work, relieved that Charles was already gone. I slid the ring off my finger and placed it in my nightstand. Until I figured out what was going on between me and Jonathan, I certainly wasn't going to go public.

I had barely settled into my office when there was a knock on my door.

"Are you okay?" Ginger asked, "You're here early this morning." She made her way fully into my office.

"Well…" I started to discuss with Ginger about what happened this weekend, but then remembered what Charles said about her gossiping and changed my mind. "Yes, I am fine, I just needed to wrap up a couple of reports."

"I'm headed to the coffee shop, do you want anything?"

"Absolutely." I gave her my order, then watched as she walked out, still tempted to confide in her. No, I decided, not yet. I'd learned over the years that it's better to keep it quiet until you know about a relationship for sure.

Twenty minutes later Ginger returned with my latte. As she placed it on my desk, I asked, "Have you seen Charles today? He isn't answering his office phone."

"Oh, he left a voicemail asking me to let you know that he had to fly to Chicago and would be there a couple of days. He sounded upset." Ginger shot me a questioning look as if I might know what was going on.

My heart started to beat fast. *Chicago? Okay Tanya, stay calm. You aren't doing anything wrong; there's no company policy about personal relationships.*

"Thanks for letting me know, Ginger. I'll touch base with him later." I smiled to let her know I was not concerned. "Thanks for the latte."

All day I was a nervous wreck, thinking that Charles would mention to Jonathan that he was staying with me or that Jonathan would mention that we got engaged. Fortunately, I had a ton of work to do, and at the end of the day I was surprised at how much I'd gotten done. Then again, I always worked well when stressed.

That night I decided to call Jonathan and ask about his day, hoping he'd say something about why Charles was in Chicago.

"Hello, you've reached Jonathan Skagel…"

I sighed in annoyance, then left him what I hoped sounded like a casual voicemail asking him to call me back. After tossing and turning in bed, I realized that sleep wasn't going to happen no time soon, so I turned on Netflix and started watching some cheesy romantic comedy. An hour later, my cellphone rang. I jumped up and grabbed the phone, then set it back down on the nightstand when I saw it was Charles. Had he found out about Jonathan? I waited until I heard the chirp indicating a new voicemail, then picked it up and pressed play.

"Hi Tanya, I was just calling to see how your weekend went. I'm sure Ginger told you I had some things to take care of in the Chicago office, but I'll be back tomorrow evening. Okay, well, have a good night."

I exhaled in relief. He sounded completely normal.

On my way home from work the following evening I decided I would tell Charles about me and Jonathan. This secrecy thing was stressing me out. I tried calling Jonathan again but there was no answer so I sent an email. I'd hoped that his disappearing acts would stop now that we were engaged, but apparently he felt differently. My intention was to stay up and wait on Charles to arrive, but the stress of everything must have exhausted me because I fell asleep on the sofa.

The next I knew I was jolted awake by a loud thump. A moment later Charles appeared, looking apologetic.

"I'm so sorry, I dropped my luggage."

"That's okay" I paused not wanting to sound anxious then continued, "Did everything go alright in Chicago?"

He gave me a curt nod in response. "Yeah, everything's alright, but Tanya, they just make me so mad. If those jerks did their job then maybe I wouldn't have to fly out there on a surprise visit to see what the hell we pay them for!"

I looked at him in surprise. I'd never heard Charles talk this way before. He was always so mellow, taking everything in stride.

He must have sensed what I was thinking because he apologized for his tone.

"No need to apologize, I've just never heard you so angry." I paused. "I thought the Chicago branch was doing well."

Charles looked at me and snickered. "I don't know why my father put Jonathan Skagel over that branch; he was definitely not my choice. After months of low numbers, he has to nerve to request to take a month off. Said the long hours are taking a toll on his marriage."

I sat up straighter on the couch, my throat tightening. Scenes from the weekend, including the moment he placed the ring on my finger, flashed through my mind.

"Jonathan's married…" I blurted out without thinking.

"Yeah, he's married." He smiled. "I know you don't like office gossip but you must have heard the rumors. Tanya, are you okay?"

I snapped out of it. "Rumors?"

"Yeah, that he's been messing around with some of the office clerks. That's the other reason I went there." He paused. "This conversation is just between us, Tanya. Tanya… earth to Tanya." He touched my arm.

"Are you sure the women aren't just lying on him?" I tried to sound casual but my heart was pounding and I was beginning to sweat.

"Oh please, he was flirting with Renee when we brought him in for the interview. I knew then that the man was trouble." Charles snorted. "He's so full of himself."

Renee was Charles' secretary and quite pretty. Had something happened between them? I was about to ask, but just then Charles touched my hand.

"You can't repeat what I'm about to tell you to anyone. Two sexual harassment charges have been initiated against him within the last six months. Since the investigations are pending, we can't fire him, but we certainly can fire him for forging numbers."

I felt like was going to throw up.

"Tanya, are you sure you're okay? You look sick…"

"Yeah, um, actually, I'm not feeling so great. I think I'm going to go lie down."

"Okay, I'll walk you up." Charles stood, then grabbed my arm and guided me to the stairs. "Let me know if you need anything during the night."

I nodded. "Thanks, Charles." Then I headed to my room, shut the door behind him, and laid across my bed.

"How stupid could I be?" I rubbed my temples. It now made sense why I could only reach him doing certain hours of the day and why he disappeared for weeks on end. I could have kicked myself for being so naive.

The next morning I couldn't move, and when Charles came to check on me I told him I wasn't feeling well and wouldn't be in today. My mind was racing as I heard him moving around downstairs. As soon as he left I sat up in the bed and opened my nightstand drawer, my gaze shifting from the nine-millimeter handgun to the small box next to it. I pulled out the box and opened it, staring at the ring Jonathan had given me less than four days ago.

He was going to be sorry he ever betrayed me.

CHAPTER 4

SYLVIA SYKES-SKAGEL

Turning the eye to a low heat, I stirred the lemon-buttered sauce for the salmon dinners from Magnolia's Steakhouse. It was my and Jonathan's favorite restaurant, always earning every one of its five stars. It's also where we had our first date.

As I pulled two champagne glasses from the cupboard my phone dinged. I glanced down at it and read the message that appeared: "Hey babe, I'm going to be late tonight."

I picked up the phone and started to reply, but stopped myself. *What's the point?* I thought.

Today was our thirteenth wedding anniversary and he had made no mention of it all day. Did he even remember? His assistant usually sent flowers for him, but this year I hadn't even received those. Still, I'd held a glimmer of hope that he would surprise me tonight with a nice gift and a bouquet of pink lilies, my favorite. Now, after reading his message, my heart was broken. I didn't know how much more disappointment I could take from him.

I had done everything to make this night special. After I dropped off our kids, ten-year-old Sophia and seven-year-old Jonathan Jr., at my parent's house, I headed to Magnolia's to pick up the food, thinking we'd have a romantic dinner at home. When the flowers didn't come, I told myself it didn't matter, that there was no way he would forget this day, especially not after I'd been dropping hints all week. I actually got excited as I took a long leisurely bath and slipped into his favorite dress. It had been a long time since we had any quality time and I was looking forward to rekindling our relationship.

Over the last three years, Jonathan and I had grown more distant than ever before. He had been taking more weekly trips and seemed to pick the conferences that required him to stay away from home. When he was in town he barely made it home before eight pm and sometimes it was closer to ten. I had even begun to question my husband's faithfulness again, and with great reason.

Five years into our marriage, I'd learned that Jonathan was carrying on several affairs. His carelessness gave him away; he purchased a handbag for one of his women and mistakenly charged it on our joint credit card. I still might not have found out because he paid all the bills, but the banking app alerted me about the expensive transaction.

I remember feeling so violated when I called the department store to report the identity theft. I remember the voice of the perky store associate who answered on the first ring. I remember how her voice changed when I explained about the notification from the app – that the card was stolen and she couldn't have followed proper protocol in checking identification.

"The man, Mr. Skagel, had his ID," she said nervously, "He said he was buying a gift for his wife."

"I *am* his wife," I stated coldly.

"Oh, Ms. Patrice, please don't let him know I told you. He wanted it to be a surprise."

Patrice? I thought, my heart in my throat. Then it came to me; she was one of the secretaries at Jonathan's firm. I'd met her at the company picnic the previous summer, which Jonathan had begged me to attend. The Accounting Firm Jonathan worked for had rented out an amusement park, and Patrice, in her cut-off booty shorts, had certainly stood out amongst the other employees and their families. When Jonathan introduced us she gave a half-assed smile and rolled her eyes. At the time I hadn't thought twice about it; having a husband who resembled actor Djimon Hounsou often made me the object of other women's envy. And it wasn't just his looks; he had a presence that drew people to him and made them listen when he spoke. Though it was exciting to be with someone so charismatic, it wasn't always easy. I'd learned long ago to overcome my own jealousy; otherwise I would have driven myself crazy. Now I realized that my faith in my marriage had really been naivete.

When Jonathan arrived home that evening I confronted him about the handbag, fully expecting him to promise never to see Patrice outside work again. Instead, he started nervously rambling about a woman by the name of *Chery.*

Chery? How many damn bags had he bought?

A huge fight ensued, and when I threatened to leave, Jonathan promised to end both relationships. I was torn because I didn't want to be a single mother of a two-year-old. I didn't want to go back to work as a dental hygienist. I didn't want to go back to living in a four-hundred-square-foot studio or, God forbid, move back in with my parents. Better yet, I didn't want the stigma of a failed marriage. I didn't want to hear their "I told you so." So, I decided to stay but only if he agreed to counseling and quit the firm he worked for.

"How can you fix our marriage while still looking at the women who are helping you destroy it?" I asked.

Jonathan reluctantly agreed. Three weeks later, he'd landed a position at Brookes Brothers.

That change, along with the counseling, seemed to work for us. In fact, things were going so well that in year eight we decided to expand our family. Unlike my first pregnancy which took two years of us trying to conceive, I got pregnant quickly. I was so happy and hoped it would strengthen our relationship even more, and it did, for a while.

When Jonathan Junior was born, it seemed like Jonathan had found this new understanding of family. He talked about the legacy he would leave for our children and wanted to be a good role model for them, especially for his son. For the first year after the baby was born, my husband came home at five every night. He was so attentive. Our daughter Sophia loved it. He would read her bedtime stories, help her with her homework, and even had time to play with her outside before it got dark. Jonathan helped me cook dinner, and even cared for the baby, which allowed me to get back into the gym. We were finally getting into our groove.

Then something changed. I don't know what happened that made Jonathan revert back to his old ways, but it started right after Jonathan Jr. turned two. Five o'clock became six, and before I knew it he wasn't coming home until eight. He made excuses about changes at work and how much pressure he was under.

"Babe, it's like I have to keep proving myself to these people," he said one night when I confronted him about coming in at ten-thirty. "And if I want to keep advancing, I have to put in the work." Then came a guilt trip he'd started laying on me for making him quit his previous job. It was "my fault" that he had to work harder and longer to support our lifestyle. I had never asked for this lifestyle. I would've been okay in a three-bedroom bungalow, in a nice neighborhood. Jonathan was the one who wanted this twenty-five-hundred-square-foot, five-bedroom home, saying we would fill all the rooms with kids. Now, three years later, I laugh at that thought. How could we fill a house with kids when he's never home to help me conceive them?

I glanced at the clock – it was now seven-forty-two – and pulled the meal out of the oven. It had been warming for over an hour now and I was becoming very hungry. I grabbed a plate and scooped the salmon and roasted veggies on it, then ladled the lemon-butter sauce over the salmon. Instead of eating at the dining room table that I decorated for the evening, I decided to eat at the kitchen bar. I grabbed a roll out of the to-go container and got the bottle of champagne I had chilling in the fridge. With each bite, I got more and more upset with Jonathan, not only for forgetting our anniversary but the fact that he could be possibly spending time with one of his whores right now.

When I was halfway finished with my dinner, Jonathan walked into the house. By then it was a quarter after eight. He walked over to me and kissed me on the forehead. There was silence. I continued to eat. He looked at my plate of food, which though half-gone was clearly fancier than the average dinner, then to the decorated dining room table, and finally the stove, where the other piece of salmon was sitting in the oven dish.

"I thought we should have something special for our anniversary," I said, then put a forkful of veggies in my mouth.

Jonathan's facial expression was that of total shock. He looked at his phone, I assumed to check the date, then exhaled heavily. A second later I felt arms go around me; he nuzzled his face against the side of my neck and held it there.

"I'm sorry" he moaned over and over again. He then pulled back, grabbed my face and tilted it up so I could look him in his eyes. "I am sorry for forgetting our anniversary."

I was shocked, Jonathan was admitting that he was wrong without blaming me for not reminding him. It was a sincere apology, and it was for more than just forgetting our anniversary. That's when I noticed the scent of a woman on him.

He pulled me up from my seat and pulled me into his arms. I was stiff for a minute, then embraced him back. I still wasn't ready to end our marriage. We stood that way for several minutes, then I gently released him, wiped my eyes and went to fix him a plate. Jonathan sat on the barstool next to mines and poured himself a glass of champagne. He tried to engage me in small chitchat but my mind wasn't there anymore; I was too busy wondering how many women he was carrying on with this time.

~ ~ ~

Jonathan flipped me over and entered from behind. After dinner, he'd changed out of his work clothes and presumably made some half-assed attempt to wipe the smell of her off him, but it lingered. It was a familiar scent, too – had been on his several times in the past two months. When I'd asked him about it the bastard would say, "It was a work social event and you know how women are."

He couldn't even look me in the eye, even though he knew that I loved looking into his eyes when made love. Finally he collapsed on me and breathed heavily on my neck. After a couple of minutes, I moved out from under him. Jonathan rolled to the other side of the bed and curled up, his breathing becoming heavy once again. I slowly got out of the bed, careful not to disturb him, and walked into the bathroom. Locking the door behind me, I turned to look at myself in the mirror with uncontrollable tears running down my face. I stood at five-foot-eight and a toned one hundred seventy pounds. I kept myself up and worked out four days a week. I touched my newly blown-out hair and the soft curls that brushed my cheek. Clearly, it wasn't good enough for him. I couldn't help but blame myself for Jonathan's infidelity, though my therapist told me it had nothing to do with me. One thing was for sure – staying in this marriage had everything to do with my growing depression.

I heard the doorknob turn and quickly wiped my eyes. Jonathan didn't knock, as soon as I heard his footsteps move away I opened the door to the shower and got in. I allowed the hot water to wash over my head and onto my body. I didn't care that I was messing up my hair that had taken three hours to get done that morning. I wanted the scent of Jonathan and that woman off me. The steam from the shower quickly filled up the room.

Twenty minutes later, I stepped out the shower and dried off. When I opened the door, Jonathan was lying in the middle of the bed, fully naked, asleep. I quietly walked out of the bedroom and downstairs to the kitchen. The clock read eleven-eleven, and I remembered reading that this number was significant, a sign to change one's perspective. I reached for the half-empty bottle of champagne on the countertop, popped the cork and turned it up and took a big gulp. I didn't bother getting a glass; I knew I would finish it off before heading back upstairs.

CHAPTER 5

VERONICA (RED) REDMOND

My partner Black and I decided to stop at our favorite Chinese spot, Mi' Sing Lay, to order takeout. I got my usual shrimp fried rice and Black got his sesame chicken. Unfortunately we didn't have a chance to eat it, because a robbery was taking place three blocks over. Detectives usually didn't handle these types of calls but we never hesitated on filling in when needed, especially if we were close by. We loved the excitement and it certainly beat being behind the desk doing paperwork. Black responded to dispatch that we were on our way while I grabbed our food and followed him out to the vehicle.

We were the first ones on the scene, and as we approached the store we saw a crowd gathered outside.

Through the windows, we could see the owner ducked behind the register, his hand gripping a shotgun. The robbers were out of sight but we knew from dispatch that they were also armed and were now probably waiting to get a clear shot. In the distance we could hear approaching sirens; our backup was on the way.

Black went around to the back of the store, while I used the squad car, a couple of street posts, and a roll of crime scene tape to create a barrier between the store and the growing onlookers. I then moved closer to get a clearer view of the suspects, my heart skipping a beat when I saw they were just teenage boys, one black and one white. I knew that if they made it out of this alive, they would be spending the next twenty years behind bars. One was hiding behind a display of Coke Products and the other one was behind the aisle that held an array of potato chips. They looked scared. I'm sure they didn't expect the owner, a black gentleman in his mid-fifties, to have a shotgun and be ready to fight back.

Captain Richard Morgan and several police officers approached the scene and quickly surrounded the store. The captain saw me and gave me a curious look, no doubt wondering why we were there.

"Black's around back," I said.

He looked upset, but nodded. He knew Black was the best person on the force to handle this type of situation. A moment later I heard his voice booming through the loudspeaker, asking everyone to put down their guns, but before he could finish a shot went off. I glanced in the store in time to see Black falling backward. He was hit!

Without hesitation, I ran into the store. "Black!"

One of the cops held me back as the other police officers charged towards the suspects and tackled them to the ground. At this point, the owner's hands were in the air. I escaped the cop's grip and ran to my partner, who was breathing heavily and tapping his chest. The vest had stopped the bullet. Exhaling with relief, I pulled the vest off him, then inspected the nasty bruise on his chest. Black winced but managed to give me a reassuring look. He was going to be okay.

I backed away so the paramedics entering the store could evaluate him. Outside the store window, I could see the suspects being loaded into the back of the squad cars. They looked terrified. A few feet away the captain was talking to the store owner while two news crews waited like buzzards to get a statement from them.

A minute later the paramedics carried Black out on a stretcher. I heard him protest a few times, but it was half-hearted. He knew that the captain wouldn't allow him back without a full checkup. With a sigh I got into the squad car and followed the ambulance to the hospital, all too aware of how close I'd come to losing my partner.

~ ~ ~

Three hours later, I walked into my house holding the bag of Chinese food from Mi' Sing Lay. After kicking my shoes off, I reached under my shirt, unhooked my bra and pulled it off. Tears flooded my face and I wasn't sure why. Was it Black's near-brush with death, or the fact that two teenage boys were in jail? What about their mother, their father, or their friends who would be losing them to the correctional facility? What about the owner? Would he be able to mentally walk into his store and continue to provide service to the community? And what about his wife or family? They might not want him to return.

I walked into my kitchen, grabbed a fork and a bottle of wine, then flopped into my favorite leather chair. Shrimp fried rice would definitely hit the spot right now. I opened the box and rolled my eyes in disgust.

"Ugh... they forgot my shrimp!!" I reached in the bag and pulled out Black's sesame chicken and began to eat it.

This is my life, I thought as I listened to the quietness of the night. I pulled the fortune cookie out the bag and cracked it open. It read, "The time is now." I laughed. *What did that even mean?* After eating a couple more bites, I put the leftovers in the fridge then headed upstairs.

I was stepping out of the shower when I heard my phone vibrate. I walked into the bedroom, dripping water on the hardwood floors as I looked for the phone, and finally found it in the back pocket of my discarded pants. I groaned when I saw it was my sister, Tiffany; she only called when she needed money. I hesitated on answering but after the drama with Black I needed the distraction. I pressed the speaker button, then laid the phone on the bed.

"So what have you gotten yourself into this time?" I said as I walked back into the bathroom to finish drying off.

"Well hello to you too, sis," Tiffany said with a crackle in her voice.

The phone went silent, so I walked to my bed and glanced down at the screen to make sure the line was still connected. It was.

"Whassup, sis? Everything okay?" I rubbed the towel down my wet leg.

"I'm getting married."

It was my turn to go silent. *Married?* I sat my partially wet body on the bed. "Wow, I didn't know you were dating anyone…"

There was another moment of silence, then she said, "I'm marrying Jeremy."

My head immediately started hurting. The only Jeremy I knew was Jeremy Lance, my ex-boyfriend. I picked up the phone and held it to my ear, as if that would make things clearer.

"Jeremy? As in my ex, Jeremy?"

"C'mon, Red, it was so long ago and –"

I cut her off. "How long have you been dating him?"

"Six months."

"SIX MONTHS!" I yelled, "Why is this first that I am hearing about this?"

"Uhh, because I knew you would overreact about it, like how you are doing now." My sister sighed heavily. "Red, I didn't know where our relationship was going when we first got together, but we are in love and we are getting married."

I didn't know what to say, so I said nothing. When Tiffany spoke again her voice had an almost cheerful lilt to it. "I would like for you to be in the wedding."

I laughed. "That's never going to happen."

"Really, Red? It's been like twenty years since you dated him, and Mom said that –"

"*Eighteen* years," I corrected. "So you and Mom have been planning this behind my back... typical."

"It's not like that, Red."

"Look Tiff, I have to go. I've had a long day and I just can't deal with this right now." I hung up the phone.

I couldn't believe my sister had kept this a secret. Jeremy was not some fantasy guy in my head; we had dated for three years, two years in high school and one after. I'd ended it shortly after starting the police academy and although it was hard I knew it was for the best. We were young and dumb, two different people on two different paths. But that didn't give Tiff the right to pick up with him, even all these years later. There was no statute of limitations on dating your sister's ex.

Tiff and I had never been close, and it wasn't just because I was five years older than her. We were never into the same things and had very different kinds of friends. She was definitely more popular with the boys – not a surprise considering she was five-five with a figure to die for. She'd gotten that from our mother, who also maintained her one-hundred-twenty-pound weight with little to no effort, while I was taller, heavier, and had to work out to keep the pounds off. Going shopping with them had always been a nightmare. I would try to fit in with them, but prissy dresses and makeup were never my thing. Don't get me wrong, I cared about my looks, but I always felt more like me in jeans and a sweatshirt. And I would take fishing or watching sports with my dad over shopping any day. I was the "boy" he never had and that was just fine with me.

Still, it hurt that my mom knew about Tiff and Jeremy, especially since she had made it a point over the years to let me know how successful he had become. It was no secret that she thought I'd made the biggest mistake breaking up with him, and every time she heard something through the grapevine she passed it along, like when he started his own successful lawn company. She had always wanted him to be part of the family and now she was finally going to get her way. Well, good for her, but I certainly wasn't going to be a part of it.

~ ~ ~

The time is now.

My eyes flew open and I looked around, wondering what had wakened me out of such a sound sleep. Then I remembered: it was that phrase from the fortune cookie, repeating over and over again, even as I dreamed that I was walking on the beach, so happy and at peace. Now wide awake, I wondered, what did it all mean? Did I need a major life change, or just a vacation?

"The time is now," I said out loud as I jumped out the bed and started to put on clothes. Then I glanced at the clock and laughed when I saw it was 4:44 a.m. *Where are you going at this hour of the morning?* I got back in my bed and pulled my journal from the bedside table. "June 15th, 2019," I wrote. "I am 37, 5'9, a size 14, and my sister is marrying my ex. I need some excitement outside of work, I need something new, I need to lose 30lbs, I need to create the life I want."

"I had nothing holding me back – no man, no kids, and no dating life to speak of – from making a change. My mother and father didn't need me here either. Both were healthy and living their best lives, Dad playing golf with his buddies at the country club nearly every day and Mom busy with her many social groups. *And now planning my sister's wedding*, I added."

"I'm going to do it… I'm going to move," I said out loud as a huge smile appeared on my face. I looked at the clock again and the smile grew even wider. I'd just made a major life decision in under thirty minutes.

I jumped out of bed again and began pacing the bedroom floor, my mind already formulating a plan. First things first, I needed to call Storm and talk to him about it. If anyone would give it to me straight, it was my mentor and former boss.

Lieutenant Leonard Storm was like a character from a movie – strong and masculine in every sense of the word, yet sensitive as well. Even at the age of sixty-five, he still had it – looks, sharpness, and major swag. I had been heartbroken when he retired six months after making me lead detective, but he'd served thirty years on the force so I couldn't be mad at that. At the end of Storm's retirement ceremony he informed me that he was also leaving Atlanta. It was a tough blow. Storm was like a second father to me, and since he and Gayle, his wife of twenty-five years, never had any children I was the closest thing he had to a daughter. Then he told me the worst news of all: Gayle had been diagnosed with stomach cancer.

"She always wanted to live in a beach house, so I'm going to give her just that," Storm stated with tears in his eyes.

Three months later, they were enjoying the small city of Contigo Island, Georgia, but their happiness was short-lived. Gayle's cancer was spreading fast, and she passed away within the year. Storm handled her death the only way he knew how: he became a consultant for the Contigo Island's Police Department.

Six months earlier, while we were having dinner at his favorite oceanside restaurant, he looked at me and said, "If you ever want to get away, I can get you a position here in a heartbeat." At first I thought he was joking, but he wasn't laughing. I wasn't ready to leave the force at the time, but a lot had changed since then.

I paused in my pacing to glance at the clock. Storm was an early riser, but I didn't want to call before he had his morning tea. I waited until six on the dot then dialed his number.

He answered on the second ring. "Hello?"

"Storm," I said, smiling at the sound of the familiar baritone voice.

"Veronica?" he asked, concern creeping into his tone, "Is everything okay?"

"Yes sir, it's me," I replied softly, "And I'm fine."

"Well then," he boomed, "to what do I owe this pleasure so early in the morning?"

"Is it too early for you? I can call back later...?"

"Veronica, I'm a creature of habit. I'd been rising at five a.m. for the last forty years, ain't nothing changed. I like to smell the air before everyone starts polluting it," Storm said with a chuckle.

I smiled again; same old Storm.

"So to what do I owe this pleasure?" he repeated. He knew I wasn't calling him at this hour just to make idle chitchat.

"I was thinking I'd come for a visit…"

"A visit, huh?" Storm always had seen right through me.

"Well, maybe more than a visit."

We wound up speaking for over an hour, discussing my plans to relocate to the area. He said it would be a great move and assured me that I would have a place there. I felt the relief wash over me. Storm had always been my voice of reason and I looked forward to working with him again.

"You have perfect timing, Veronica," he said, then informed me that he'd recently been made Acting Chief of Police since the current chief was out on leave after a major operation.

I couldn't believe how with just one phone call everything seemed to be falling into place. Now the hard part would be convincing my current lieutenant to allow me to transfer. When I said as much to Storm, he offered to put in a call and request a transfer. Again, I sighed in relief. With Storm by my side I was hoping the lieutenant wouldn't put up too much of a fight.

CHAPTER 6

TANYA L. JAMESON

I laid in bed, looking at the ring that Jonathan had given me less than a week ago. I hadn't spoken to him since Charles informed me that he was married with kids. Knowing that Charles and Ginger would see that something was seriously bothering me, I'd called in sick for the last three days so I could avoid any questions while I figured out what to do. Yesterday had been the worst – I had literally felt sick and stayed in the bathroom most of the day, praying I wasn't pregnant, too scared to take a test.

Charles was sweet; he cooked every day and brought me fresh flowers. I told him that I had really bad cramps, knowing he'd understand because his sister had dealt with similar symptoms. I felt bad for lying, but it was better than the humiliation I'd feel if Charles knew what Jonathan had done to me. A simple google search on the man and I would've known; then again, I'd been so infatuated with him who knows if I would've believed it? After all, I'd accepted his marriage proposal within ten weeks of meeting and after he'd ghosted me for two! I'd never even met his family or his friends. I couldn't believe I got so wrapped up in him that I lost all my common sense.

Jonathan, who had no idea that I knew about his wife and kids, had continued to call and text every day. Not knowing what to say, I ignored him for two days then finally texted him that I wasn't feeling well. He asked if I needed anything and even offered to come see me. Of course I told him no; while a face-to-face confrontation was appealing in theory, the truth was I didn't know what I would do if I saw him.

The chime of my front door alarm startled me out of the bed. I knew it was Charles, coming to check on me during lunch. I couldn't believe I had stayed in bed so long. Before he left that morning I'd told him I was feeling a little better and would go downstairs to eat the breakfast he had made; here it was four hours later and I was in the same spot.

I was slipping into my robe when I heard a light knock on my door.

"Tanya, are you up?" I opened the door to find Charles standing there with a concerned look on his face.

"I'm fine, just having a slow start today."

"I noticed... you didn't eat your breakfast," he said. "Tanya, I can stay a couple more days." Charles had planned on moving back to his condo later on today.

"It's fine... I'm fine," I said softly, "I will be okay in a day or so."

Charles walked over and wrapped his arms around me. His embrace was so tight and comforting that I found myself relaxing into it. Neither of us spoke for a moment, then he pulled away awkwardly.

"Well, I guess I better get going..." Charles narrowed his eyes at me. "If you're sure you're okay."

I smiled. "Yes."

The smile remained in place until I heard him leave. Then I let the robe drop to the floor, got back into bed and let the tears come once more.

A couple of hours later, I woke to the sound of kids playing. I sat up in my bed and glanced out the window. Ms. Caldwell, an older black woman who lived next door, was sitting in a chair on her back patio, watching her grandkids jump in and out of the pool. I smiled seeing the excitement on the kids' faces, but that just reminded me of the kids I'd imagined me and Jonathan having. I exhaled and reached over to the nightstand to grab my laptop. As I typed in my password, I thought of a way to seek my revenge on Jonathan. He had taken a lot from me, not just my dignity but my hopes of a life with him. Maybe it was time to make him pay for it.

CHAPTER 7

VERONICA REDMOND

Lieutenant Richard Morgan wasn't happy when I submitted my transfer papers. I couldn't blame him either; the transfer request was totally unexpected. He told me that it usually takes months for approval, but I didn't have months to wait. I had been feeling trapped for a while, and the incident with Black had made me realize that life was precious and that every minute of it should be enjoyed.

The lieutenant's tone went from surprised to furious when I mentioned my plans to work with Storm. He reiterated how long the process took and demanded that I stayed until he replaced me. No way, I thought; it could take him six months to find a replacement … maybe longer. I knew Morgan's anger was directed more towards Storm than me. Ever since Storm had left, Morgan had been trying desperately to fill his very large shoes, and he was failing. Storm had thirty years on the force, compared to Morgan's twenty. Storm was tall, in great shape, and made it a point to get to know a little about everyone's personal life. Morgan was short, stocky, and could stand to lose fifty pounds, plus he didn't care to know anything about us, he just wanted us to do our job. Now it looked like he would be losing one of his best detectives to Storm and it was the straw the broke the camel's back. I knew Storm thought of them as friends, and I didn't have the heart to let him know that Morgan didn't feel the same way.

Two days before I was to leave I called Storm to make sure everything was set on his end. Instead, he told me that he had never received the paperwork from my precinct. I was angry, mostly at myself. I'd been so caught up in packing and other details of the move that I hadn't checked the status; I should have known Morgan would try to sabotage things. I glanced at the clock, then pulled out my phone again. It was late in the evening but I knew he would still be in the office.

Morgan answered on the third ring. When I questioned him about the paperwork he said something about it being held up in HR. I played along with him but as soon as we hung up I called Sarah, the head of HR. Sarah and I had been close friends for about two years, ever since we'd caught the same elevator at the end of a long day and decided to go out for drinks. A few hours and many laughs later, we'd left the bar feeling like we had known each other forever. We never did go out drinking again, but we always knew we could count on each other. We spent a few minutes catching up, then I asked about the paperwork. Sarah expressed surprise that I was leaving, this confirmed my suspicions: the paperwork hadn't been submitted. Clearly, Morgan was going to make this as difficult as possible.

The next morning I headed to the Human Resources office to talk to Sarah face to face. I had no sooner entered her office when she raised a set of paperwork in the air, saying it had been on her desk when she got to work. When I told her of my plans to leave the following day, she explained that the transfer had yet to be accepted and that I'd been premature in making arrangements. I couldn't argue with her; I knew it had been presumptuous of me to think that I could walk in, ask for a transfer, and be granted one just like that.

"What can I do?" I asked her.

Sarah got up from her desk and closed the office door. "Well, if I recall correctly about a month ago you took a couple of sick days." I nodded. "And I saw that you had quite a bit of sick time."

"Sarah, where are you going with this?"

"I will put a rush on your transfer paperwork."

"That's great," I began, but she held up a hand. "It still may take a while, like a month maybe two."

I sighed. "That long?"

"Yes, that long, but if you can get a letter from your doctor I can put you on immediate administrative leave due to stress. Since we don't have records of why you took off last month, we can show a track record that will validate the administrative leave. Can you get me a letter by tomorrow?"

I stood up and smiled. "I can get you a letter by the end of the day. Thanks, Sarah." I gave her a light hug and walked out of her office.

CHAPTER 8

VERONICA REDMOND

I took a big gulp of my vodka and cranberry cocktail then closed my eyes as the plane ascended into the air. I was pleased that the flight wasn't full and that I was able to snag a first-class seat with the blessings of the captain himself. Seeing my detective's badge always gave the flight staff a sense of security and I was well compensated for it, with upgraded seats, free meals, free drinks – you name it, I could get it. I exhaled, still not able to believe this was happening, and so soon. A smile quickly replaced the worry in my mind as I glanced out the window at the clouds.

"I can't believe I will be finally living close to the ocean," I said softly. I had always dreamt of waking up to the sound of the waves every morning and taking long walks on the beach, but I had never really believed it could happen. It was certainly not on my radar when I joined the Kennesaw Police Department at the age of twenty.

I'd know from the time I was a little girl that I wanted to be a detective. Mostly it was because my dad was the Chief of Police and I wanted to follow in his footsteps. After high school, I enrolled in community college as an Education major in an attempt to appease my mother, but after a year I dropped out and entered the police academy. Mom wasn't happy about it.

"Why would you want to spend all day in that tacky uniform, chasing criminals and getting dirty? You're just like your father."

I took that as a compliment, and I enjoyed every minute of my work. I took every certification course the force offered in order to advance my career, and with guidance from my dad I gained the knowledge and earned the respect of my colleagues. Yet I knew I couldn't stay in Kennesaw forever; if I did I would always be in his shadow and I wanted to earn detective on my own merit.

After five years with the Kennesaw Police Department, I moved to Atlanta to join their force. Atlanta was less than an hour away, but the city was big enough that I could pave my own way. And I did. By the time I was thirty I had made detective and three years later I made Lead Detective. Now thirty-seven, I found myself exhausted and burnt out. Crime scenes, uncooperative witnesses, in-denial family members and endless paperwork had all taken their toll. Dad had always made this life look so glamorous, but maybe that was because he was my hero. Now I saw things in a different light. Dad popped pills for high blood pressure, high cholesterol and anxiety, and he rarely came home before seven. I didn't get it when I was little because he made sure he was there to tuck me and my sister in every night, but after he closed our door, I would hear my parents fight about how his job was going to kill him and destroy our family. He had finally retired four years ago, the same year I made Lead Detective.

Now I was on a plane headed to Southern Georgia, where the crime is low, and the margaritas are constant, hoping to lead a different life. Hoping I'd have enough chill time to finally finish that painting that I'd been working on for the last five years. Maybe I would take up yoga. A smile appeared on my face as the plane descended. *I made it, I am finally here.*

Storm had said he would pick me up from the airport, and I turned on my phone so I could call and let him know I'd landed. As it came to life, the phone began dinging, notifying me of messages.

"Wow, someone really missed you," a deep male voice with a thick, unfamiliar accent came from over my shoulder.

As the seatbelt light went off, everyone started to stand. I unbuckled my seatbelt, stood and noticed a very handsome black gentleman retrieving a carryon from the compartment. I smirked and looked at my phone, which was still beeping. I switched it to silent, then looked and noticed five voicemails – two from my mom, two from my sister, and one from Storm. I also had seven text messages, all from my sister. Knowing that my family would try to talk me out of moving, I'd waited 'til yesterday to drive to my parents' house to tell them. My new city is only five hours away, I said, and they could visit anytime they wanted to. They listened to my carefully prepared, five-minute speech on why this was a great decision, then they started in on the negative about a woman traveling alone and living in a strange place. I'd thought the fact that Storm was there would ease their minds, especially since they'd always been so fond of him, but that wasn't the case.

"But he isn't family," my dad stated.

After unsuccessfully trying to convince them, I kissed and hugged my parents and walked out the door. I was still upset with my sister, so I didn't bother telling her, hence the multiple messages and text message. I knew she would be pissed, but I didn't have time to listen to those messages.

I pressed the voice message from Storm. "Red, a big case just landed on my lap and it's pretty bad. I'm on my way to the crime scene now; looks like you came just in time. I'm sending a patrol officer to pick you up and bring you to the site, I hope you're ready to work."

Storm only called me Red when he was stressed out and in business mode. I grunted and said, "Noooooo!" out loud before I realized it.

"It can't be that bad," the handsome gentleman said to me as I slumped back in my seat. I let the other passenger that was sitting by me cross over me.

"This was supposed to be vacation work," I said and looked at the man, who was now standing in the aisle with about five people behind him gawking. He laughed and said, "No such thing as vacation work."

I noticed his thick accent again and tried to place where he was from. He grabbed his carry-on bag and nodded at me, then walked towards the exit door.

My eyes followed him. *Well, there goes my early mornings, watching the sunrise, while eating breakfast.* I waited until everyone deplaned, then slowly stood up, grabbed my bag, and made my way down the aisle. I was not ready for this.

Storm must have given the patrol officer a description of me, because as I approached baggage claim 11 to retrieve my luggage he approached and introduced himself as Officer Luis. He was a Latino male no more than thirty years old, with a pleasant but focused demeanor. We waited there in silence, his eyes automatically flicking about, taking note of everyone in the area.

After five minutes the light started flashing and the belt started moving. I felt the eyes of someone watching me and glanced up to see the handsome gentleman from the plane staring directly at me. He nodded to Officer Luis standing beside me and smilingly mouthed, "Are you in trouble?" I smiled back and nodded my head, "Yes." I was jolted out of my air conversation by Officer Luis asking me to point to my bag. I looked at the carrousel and noticed the blue ribbon I'd tied to the handle of my black suitcase to easily identify it.

"That one," I said, louder than I wanted to, and pointed to it. Officer Luis grabbed my suitcase and headed to the SUV that was parked right out front. I glanced over my shoulder, hoping to make eye contact again with the handsome gentleman, but he was busy helping an older lady retrieve her suitcase from the moving carousel.

Well that fairytale was fun for a moment, I thought, *now back to reality.*

I arrived at the crime scene and immediately spotted Storm. He was letting his gray beard grow out and looked even more distinguished than I remembered. I thanked Officer Luis for the ride and headed toward Storm. He saw me and gave a reassuring smile, then enveloped me in a hug.

"Come, meet the rest of the team," he said.

The "rest of the team" turned out to be just two other people. There was Chief Alexander, a tall, James Evans from Good Times type of guy, who was still recovering from his surgery. He seemed more like an English teacher than the Chief. On the other hand, Deputy Gomez, a five-foot-two Latina woman, looked like she was more at home at a crime scene than in her own house. This was her territory.

Deputy Gomez and Chief Alexander shook my hand, then got right back to business. Storm stated that he would bring me up to speed, so for the moment we stayed several feet from the crime scene.

I glanced over at the covered body. "Have they identified the victim?"

"Not yet," Storm stated. "A couple of joggers spotted the body and called us. What we do know is that she is an African American woman around five-foot-six and married – or at least she's wearing a wedding band. There appears to be no sexual assault, but we won't know for sure until the body is fully examined."

"So why hasn't the body been picked up by the lab?" I asked.

"Because I haven't released it," a strong male voice with a thick accent walked up behind us.

I glanced around to see the handsome man from the plane.

"We meet again." He held out his hand for me to shake. "I'm Special Agent Christophe."

"You two know each other?" Storm asked, sounding more protective than curious.

"Detective Redmond," I said as I accepted the hand. *Nice grip.* "FBI? Why is the FBI here?"

Before I got my answer, Chief Alexander walked up. "You must be from the FBI," he said to Christophe, "The body is over here."

I glanced at Storm as the two walked away. "What's going on?"

"This isn't the first body," he stated and diverted his eyes.

"WHAT?" I said, almost screaming, then lowered my voice – no need to make a scene at a crime scene. "How could you keep this from me? We talked a couple of days ago and you mentioned nothing about this, plus you knew – "

Storm held up his hand and quietly said, "Not here, not now, later, okay?"

I nodded and he took my hand and guided me to where the team stood talking.

"Nice of you two to join us," Deputy Gomez said with a side smile.

"So her body is in the same position as the last victim," Special Agent Christophe said to no one in particular.

He walked around to the left side of the victim and held her arm up. He pointed to a tiny needle mark, under her left armpit. "Same needle entry." He stood back up and looked at us. "I believe we could have a potential serial killer on the loose."

I glanced at Storm. I couldn't believe he'd gotten me caught up in this.

Special Agent Christophe gave the orders to the uniformed officers on how to bag the crime scene and instructed the medical examiner to take the body. Then the four of us walked with him towards his vehicle.

Halfway there he said, "I'll be in touch soon. Please let me know when the autopsy comes in." Though he was speaking to Chief Alexander, he was looking at me.

I glanced away, not knowing what to think of his piercing stare. Once he'd finished speaking to Chief Alexander, he said to me, his tone suddenly sharp, "Are you new to this?"

This man has some nerve! I glanced at the others to see if they had heard, but they were speaking amongst themselves. Somehow managing to hide my annoyance, I met his gaze and firmly said, "No."

"Okay. You seemed a bit taken back and I just wanted to ensure that we have the best working on this. I won't have a third body on my watch."

"I'm fine and I can handle this," I said coldly.

"Good to hear," he stated then turned and got in his vehicle.

I took a deep breath and started walking toward the others as they were making their way back to the crime scene, then stopped. I was shaken and confused and needed a minute. I scanned the series of police cruisers parked along the street, then found what I was looking for: Storm's classic Grand Marquis and begin walking towards it. The door was unlocked so I got in and waited for him to finish with Chief Alexander. I watched as the setting sun was suddenly covered by the dark clouds forming and thought how I would have loved seeing this on the Ocean my first night here. My plan was to demand that Storm drive me straight to the airport so I could get my ass back on the plane. But as Storm approached the vehicle, I saw the look on his face and realized he needed me; otherwise he never would've done this. He needed me and I owed him everything.

I stayed quiet as he got in, cranked up the car and slowly pulled away. We drove in silence for about two miles, then he pulled over and killed the engine.

He glanced at me. "Veronica," he said in a tone I'd never heard before, "I'm sorry. I should've told you, but I needed someone here that I could trust."

My eyes widened.

He put up his hand. "No, no, no, I don't want you to think the worst. I work with great people, but me and you, we have history and I trust you with my life. I didn't intend to mislead you. The first killing was two weeks ago; it was of a tourist and we thought it to be a random act of crime until this body appeared this morning."

I nodded. "Okay, Storm."

"Thanks, Veronica." He exhaled and began driving again, this time toward my Airbnb. I listened silently as he gave me further details, noting how similar the crimes were. It piqued my interest. Then he fell silent and the only sound was the light raining hitting the windshield.

It was dark by the time we reached the Airbnb.

"I'll get your bags," Storm said as he got out of the car.

My bags! With everything going on I had forgotten all about them; now I realized Officer Luis must have put them in Storm's trunk when he dropped me at the crime scene. While he retrieved them my eyes scanned the rainy night. The place was very quiet, and remote, sitting on three acres of land with a lake. I looked forward to taking a walk around the property in the morning.

Storm escorted me into the house where I spotted two trays on the kitchen counter. There were various cheeses, fruit and meats and an assortment of cookies on the others. My stomach growled at the sight of it.

"I thought you would be hungry when you got off the plane," Storm said. "The cookies were hot," he glanced at his watch, "about four hours ago."

"It's fine," I said, smiling. "And yes, I'm starving. Thank you."

I glanced over to the green flowered clock on the wall; it was 8:36 p.m. but it felt like midnight. Storm saw me yawning and got the message. "I'll give you a call in the morning," he said, then gave me a quick hug.

"Please, not before six."

He smiled. "Okay, I can do that."

Once he was gone I didn't know which to do first – shower, eat or just go straight to bed. I was about to grab a piece of cheese when the vibration of my phone jolted me. My parents. I had forgotten to call and tell them I'd gotten in safely. I pulled it out of my jean pocket, and sure enough it was their home phone. I wanted to answer but didn't know if I was going to get my dad, my mom or my sister on the other line. I held my breath and pressed the green icon on my phone.

"Hello?" I said in the cheeriest voice I could muster.

"Sweetie," my dad's deep voice came through the other end. I exhaled and smiled. Out of all the three, I'd hoped it would be him.

"Hi, Dad…"

"Red, I've been worried since you didn't call."

"I know… I'm sorry, I went to work as soon as I got off the plane. So much for peace."

"Oh no, sweetie, sorry to hear that. I was hoping you would get some rest for a while. What was it… a thief?"

"A murder - two of them, in fact. They think we may have a serial killer on the loose." I regretted the words as soon as they left my lips.

"What! I can't believe Storm has you in this mess!"

"I know, Daddy," I said, trying to sound calm, but my dad continued to rant about Storm and how he knew it wasn't a good idea for me to be here. I knew I had to butt in or he would go on for at least another ten minutes.

"I'm okay and just got to the AIRBNB. I'm hungry and exhausted. I will call you tomorrow. Please tell Mom I said hello. I love you."

"Okay," he said reluctantly, "Love you too, sweetheart, be careful."

Deciding I needed a shower first, I found the bathroom, which was large and quite lovely. Twenty minutes later, I returned to the kitchen feeling refreshed and ready to address the constant growling in my stomach. I opened the fridge and saw a bottle of my favorite wine, chilled. Storm knew me so well. I grabbed the bottle and headed to the counter. I poured a glass and sat back in the chair. As I reached for a cheese square, my phone started vibrating.

"Nooo… what now?" I said out loud. I glanced at the bright screen and saw a number I didn't recognize. I immediately answered. "Hello?"

"Detective," a strong accented voice came through my phone, I immediately sat up straight.

"Yes…?"

"Sorry for calling so late, this is Special Agent Christophe."

Despite his earlier rudeness I found myself smiling. "How can I help you, Agent?"

"I got your number from Detective Storm; I hope that is okay."

"It's fine."

The line was quiet for a moment, then he said, "I just wanted to apologize for my comment this evening. I didn't mean to insinuate that you weren't qualified to be on this case; in fact, I've read about your work and think you would have brought a lot to this investigation."

Wow, I thought to myself, *handsome and knows how to apologize.*

"Are you still there?" he asked.

"Yes, I'm here and I appreciate you stating that, but what do you mean by *would have* brought to this investigation."

"I was just made aware that your transfer hasn't fully gone through yet," he said.

I took another sip of wine as the worry crept into my mind. "I know that. There was a delay in the paperwork so I am working currently as a consultant until everything has been worked out. Storm assured me that this wouldn't be a problem."

"Well it wouldn't be a problem if you were knocking on doors serving warrants, but this is a murder investigation and I need everything to be by the book. The fact that you were at my crime scene earlier could've already compromised my case," he continued, "and I can't have that."

He paused as if waiting for me to argue, but I said nothing. I was too shocked.

"I would be happy to bring you on when your transfer is completed, but I cannot take that chance right now."

When I still didn't say anything, he said, "Have a nice night Detective Redmond, I'll be in touch." Then Special Agent Christophe hung up the phone.

Why hadn't I said anything, pled my case? "Because it wouldn't have done any good," I added aloud.

As soon as I placed my phone on the counter, it vibrated again. I knew even before I looked that it was Storm.

"I know," I said quietly before he could speak, "I'm off the case."

"Damn it, I was hoping to call you before Christophe did. He had no right!" Storm was pissed.

"It's okay, I need to get settled in anyway."

Storm was quiet.

"Storm, can I call you tomorrow?"

"Sure, Red. Have a good night."

Hoping it was the last call of the evening, I sat back and popped the cheese square in my mouth and leaned back in the chair.

CHAPTER 9

TANYA L. JAMESON

The sound of sirens blaring outside dragged me from sleep. I had been sleeping so soundly, the best sleep I had gotten in a while, and I wanted to get back to it. The cool breeze wafted in through the open window and flowed across my naked body.

With a groan I pulled the covers over my head, hoping the sirens would fade away; instead they grew louder until they sounded like they were right outside my window. I jumped out of the bed, thinking that something had happened to one of my neighbors. I put on my pajama bottoms and my tattered Harris-Stowe State University sweatshirt and headed downstairs. As I walked down the stairs, my pace slowed when I noticed that the flashing lights were right outside my house.

Three officers were getting out and approaching my front door. My heart started to race. What if something had happened to my mom or dad?

I started for the door, then hesitated as I thought about all the times in the last several years when innocent black people had been gunned down by the police in their own homes.

A loud banging noise shook my front door, followed by a male's voice. "Ms. Jameson, POLICE, open the door!"

I took a deep breath and slowly opened the door. A bright light blinded my eyes, making it hard for me to see the faces behind it.

The man spoke again. "Are you Tanya Jameson?"

I put my hands to my eyes, trying to cover the light that continued to blind me.

"I said, are you Tanya Jameson?"

I replied, "Yes" and was suddenly forced to the ground by several police officers.

"Don't move!" the voice shouted in my ear, I felt the heavy weight of the officers on my back. Tears began to well up in my eyes. I wanted to say something but couldn't; I wanted to breathe but couldn't. I felt the cold metal objects cover my wrists. They were handcuffing me, but why?

One of the officers swiftly yanked me up from the ground with such force I immediately got a headache. I looked down at my Harris-Stowe sweatshirt and noticed how the light grey was becoming darker from the tears that rained down my face. As they marched me from my home, one of the officers mirandized me, though I still didn't know what for. When I got outside, I opened my eyes and saw my neighbors gathered in a circle talking and pointing at me. An officer was speaking to Ms. Caldwell, asking her God knows what.

"Tanya Jameson, you are being arrested in connection with the murder of Jonathan Skagel."

My eyes went from my neighbors to the officer that was speaking to me. I stared into the officer's face. He was a young white male, had to be no older than thirty and was wearing an ill-fitting brown suit.

"Jonathan's dead?" I whimpered. Then, before I could say anything else a black female uniformed officer approached me and whispered, "Don't say another word… You need to get a lawyer."

I looked at her as tears flooded my eyes. *You need to get a lawyer*, I repeated in my head. I couldn't believe this was happening to me.

I lowered my head as one of my neighbors pulled out his cellphone and began recording, and was almost relieved when the young detective opened the back door of the police cruiser and eased me inside. I noticed the black female police officer sitting in the front passenger seat. She didn't look my way. The detective got in the driver's seat directly in front of me and cranked up the car. He glanced at me in the rearview mirror and I looked at him, giving direct eye contact. He diverted his eyes and backed out of my driveway. I turned my head to peer out of the window. *Good thing they're tinted* I thought as we passed my neighbors pointing and gawking at the cruiser. I wished Charles was still at my place so he had been there to witness all of this.

The drive to the police station felt so surreal. I kept blinking as if trying to wake up from a nightmare. There was no way Jonathan was dead; no way had they actually thought I killed him. Then I felt the handcuffs around my wrist and realized this was all very real. I felt so naked without my cell phone or ID; I didn't even have underwear on.

When we got to the station the black female officer – I heard someone call her Officer Dawkins – took me to be processed, she was kind and instructed me on what to do. I didn't know who she was or why she was being nice to me, but I was appreciative. I would rather deal with her than the white cops who had thrown me down on the ground like I was an animal. She guided me to a large room with an old wooden desk and two chairs in the corner. There was a laptop on one end of the table. She motioned for me to sit in the chair further from the computer, then she grabbed my wrists, unlocked the right handcuff and attached it to the side of the chair. I began to circle my free wrist and that's when I noticed the diamond ring. I had just placed it back on my finger the night before during one of my bouts of crying. I stared at it, then placed my hand in my lap.

Officer Dawkins took a seat behind the computer and started typing on her laptop. After politely answering all of her questions – my name, address, social security number, and next of kin, I looked at her and asked, "Why am I here? Why am I being arrested? I didn't do anything…"

She looked at me with saddened eyes but didn't say a word, just continued typing.

Once she was done, she removed the cuff from the chair and pulled me up. "Time to get fingerprints and take your picture," she stated. I laughed inside at her choice of the word "picture" when what she really meant was my mugshot. She had me remove my ring and she placed it in a manila envelope. After being fingerprinted, I went into a room to be stripped-searched which was the most humiliating thing ever. I cried the entire time.

As I left the searching room, I looked around for Dawkins and spotted her talking to the young detective who had read me my rights. She glanced my way and started walking towards me. When she approached, I quietly asked if she could provide me with some underwear.

She looked at me, noticed I was braless, and nodded.

"Can I get my phone call now?"

She nodded again and said, "Remember, don't say anything, just ask for your lawyer." But instead of leading me to a phone, she led me to another room with a table and two chairs, one on each side of the table. She sat me in the chair furthest away from the door, then took the metal cuffs off my hand before leaving. I'd watched enough CSI and Law and Order to know that this was the interrogation room.

I rubbed my wrist, noticing the thick red marks from the cuffs, then laid my head on the table and exhaled. I was mentally and physically exhausted, but my mind was racing. I thought about one of the recent conversations I'd had with Jonathan:

"Tanya, what's going on? I have been calling and calling," he'd said, sounding concerned.

"I haven't been feeling well," I lied. Though I was disgusted with him I truly loved this man. Once I told him what I knew about him our relationship would be over; I would have to admit that it had all been a lie and I wasn't ready for that.

"Tanya, sweetie, something is going on. I can feel it." He paused. "Are you pregnant?"

"NO!" I exclaimed.

"Then what is it?"

I took a deep breath. "Is there something you want to tell me?"

"Like what?"

"Like about your life, your living situation."

"Tanya, I don't know where all of this is coming from. Who have you been talking to? I just proposed to you, we should be planning our life together, not arguing about nothing."

"This isn't nothing! Why won't you answer me? Why have I never been to your home?"

"You coming to my home has never been an issue before."

"I trusted you before."

He made an exasperated sound. "Tanya, I can't do this with you now."

"Jonathan, I can't do this at all." Tears streamed down my face as I hung up the phone.

The door opened to the interrogation room and my head snapped up; I wiped my tear-covered face with the sleeve of my sweatshirt. Two detectives came in, the young one with the oversized suit and a well-dressed older white guy, clean-shaven with a tailored-made suit and expensive cufflinks. The older one spoke first.

"Ms. Jameson, I'm Detective Hodges and this is Detective Boatman." Hodges pointed to the younger guy, who remained standing by the door, then he took the seat across from the table from me. Without further preamble, he then launched into a series of questions about my relationship with Jonathan and my whereabouts two days ago. Scared and confused, I was about to start answering when I remembered what Officer Dawkins, told me. I opened my mouth and said, "I want to call my lawyer." Detective Hodges ignored me and continued his line of questioning, stating that if I didn't have anything to hide, there was no need for a lawyer. I *didn't* have anything to hide; then again, I knew that they wouldn't have come to my house and taken me out in cuffs unless they had something on me. "I want my phone call. Now." Then I burst into tears and laid my head on the table.

Hodges angrily got up and walked out the door, followed by Boatman. My head remained glued to the table. Thirty minutes later, the door opened, and to my great relief it was Officer Dawkins. She walked over to me, told me to stand up and to put my hands behind my back. She must have noticed the red rings on my wrist, because the handcuffs were looser this time. With a sympathetic nod, she guided me out of the room and to an open space with several desks manned by officers. She sat me in a wooden chair next to what I presumed was her desk and handcuffed my left hand to it, then reached for the phone and placed it in front of me.

"Make your call," she said, then she got up and walked away from her desk. My gaze followed her until she made her way through the busy squad room then disappeared down the hallway. Then I picked up the receiver and dialed the only number I knew by heart: my parents. I was nervous as the phone rang for the fourth time. Like me, my parents still had a landline with no caller ID; what if they didn't answer? What if they weren't home?

"Come on… pick up," I whispered, tapping my feet.

The phone stopped ringing and I heard my mother's quiet sleepy voice come across the line.

"Hello?"

Tears immediately swelled in my eyes. "Ma," I rasped, then cleared my throat. "Ma, it's me."

"Tanya, baby what's wrong?" she said, and I could hear rustling in the background. Then I heard my dad's voice, "What is it, Joyce?"

"Tanya, I have your dad here, I am going to put you on speaker."

I couldn't believe this was happening. I had never given my parents any trouble, had never gotten so much as a speeding ticket; now at thirty-seven years old I was calling them in the middle of the night to post my bail!

"I'm in jail!" I cried, "They are accusing me of murdering Jonathan."

"Who the hell is Jonathan?" my dad asked.

"Please, Dad, I don't have much time to talk. I need a lawyer, I'm at Saint Louis Police Station South Precinct. Please help me." I burst into fresh tears.

Just then Officer Dawkins arrived back at the desk, sat down in front of me and tapped her watch.

"Ma, I have to go," I said.

"Don't worry, baby girl, I will take care of this," my dad said.

As I hung up the phone, Officer Dawkins placed a white paper bag on the desk and gestured for me to open it. Inside was a plain white bra and a pair of white panties.

"Thank you."

She nodded, grabbed the bag and stood up. "I have to take you to the holding cell now." She removed the left handcuff from the wooden chair and placed it back on my wrist.

She led me down the long hallway. We passed by several cells that held an array of people. Some looked like prostitutes; others appeared to be half drunk. I thanked God as we continued past those cells. We got to the end of the long hallway to an empty cell and she motioned for me to enter. As I stepped over the threshold of the cell, she took the bra and panties out of the bag and placed them in my hand, then took off the handcuffs. I heard the cell door shut behind me, then the sound of her footsteps retreated down the long hallway. I stood in the cold room, which had to be a quarter of the size of my bedroom, not knowing what to do next. It had a twin-size bed with a thin mattress, a sink and a toilet. At least I didn't have to share this space with anyone. I walked over to the bed, placed the bra and panties to the side, sat down, and cried.

Yelling broke through my dream. "Breakfast!" followed by a clanking noise. I rubbed my eyes, then bolted up as I remembered where I was. This was real. I stared into the eyes of a uniformed white policewoman in her mid-forties.

"Well do you want it or not?" she said pushing the tray through the perfectly squared hole in the metal door. I walked over to the door, grabbed it, and said, "Thank you."

"Oh, we have a polite one... let me know if you want seconds, hon," she said in a softer tone then moved to the next cell.

I looked at the plate. There was no way I wanted seconds of this: powdered eggs, a greasy sausage patty, three wilted strawberries, two pieces of toast with jelly and a carton of orange juice. I looked at the clock that hung on the wall in the hallway, it was now 7 a.m. In the wee hours of the morning I'd heard one of the prostitutes in the cell next to mine say that lawyers aren't allowed to come before eight.

Just one more hour and I will be out of here, I thought. At least I hoped so. I prayed that my dad was able to contact a lawyer for me. Looking at the tray of food, I decided to eat the toast with the grape jelly. Thirty minutes later, the same uniformed officer came around to collect our plates. I asked for water and she pointed to my sink. That's when I noticed the plastic cup beside it. Letting the water run for a minute, I placed the plastic cup underneath and took a sip of water and exhaled. I sat on the bed, frequently squinting at the clock on the wall down the hall. Eight o'clock came, then nine, then ten. At noon, the same officer came around with lunch. This time we had turkey burgers and broccoli. Ravenous, I ate all of the turkey burger then laid back down on the bed, exhausted from the effort.

At one-thirty Officer Dawkins tapped on my cell, startling me from sleep, then noisily slid the door open.

"Your lawyer is here," she said.

Finally, this nightmare is over. I walked over to the door, turned around and put my hands together for her to cuff me. It's amazing how quickly you learn the rules of jail.

Officer Dawkins smiled and said, "No need for that, you're being released."

I was so excited I wanted to hug her but knew that might not be a good idea. I didn't know who my parents had called and I didn't care – whoever it was getting me out of here. We walked down the long hallway and I spotted a short, balding, older black gentleman talking to Detective Hodges. He was holding a manila folder in his hand. As we approached he looked at me and nodded. That's when I realized who he was – a deacon from my parents' church.

As I approached, I said, "Thank you."

He touched my hand and squeezed it, then pulled paperwork from the envelope, signed it, and led me out of the police station. As soon as we stepped outside I spotted my parents. They quickly walked towards me and wrapped their arms around me. I wasn't expecting to see them but was so happy that they were here. They must have headed my way as soon as I called and drove all morning, picking up the deacon on the way. We all got into Dad's SUV and headed to my house.

"How did I get bail?" I asked, because I didn't think that was the norm for a murder charge.

"They didn't have anything solid to hold you on," the deacon replied matter-of-factly.

"What!" I exclaimed. "Then why the hell did I spend the night in that place ?"

"Because you are a person of interest so they were able to hold you for up to twenty-four hours, but that's it." He looked at me and despite his calm demeanor I could tell his anger matched my own. "They were completely out of line arresting you like that. When I spoke to the lead detective on the case, I learned they did not even have an arrest warrant. Rest assured the District Attorney is going to be hearing from me on this. Their case against you has taken a major hit." He placed his hand on mine. "But Tanya, you aren't in the clear. They still have you high on their radar for this and will try to charge you. We have to start building your defense."

My gaze moved from the deacon to the front seat where my parents exchanged nervous glances. My mother reached back and touched my hand. "We will get through this, Tanya."

For the rest of the ride I glared out the window, thinking about Jonathan, his wife and kids, all his lies, and my job. I didn't know how I was going to get out of this. I was quickly pulled from my thoughts as my dad pulled on my street. Several of my neighbors were outside, talking to each other. I'm sure they were spreading the news about me, the local "criminal." My yard looked a hot mess from where the police cars had pulled onto the lawn, which was wet from the constant rain that poured over the city the last several days.

Everyone stared as my dad pulled into the driveway and we got out of the SUV, but I didn't look their way. I just grabbed my dad's arm and followed him into the house. Once we got inside, I turned to him and cried as he held me.

CHAPTER 10

VERONICA REDMOND

It had been four days since I arrived in Contigo Island and aside from a killer being on the loose, things had been going well. I hadn't realized how stressed I was until I wasn't. And right now, I wasn't. I took a walk on the beach every day, my gun was tucked safely in the holster on my waist. And I was finally putting to use the techniques I'd learned at a meditation retreat a couple of years ago. I was practicing focusing my thoughts on the positive and doing quite well, though it was hard not to focus on the case that had the entire city in fright.

Storm kept me abreast of some aspects of the case, and I had to admit I was feeling a rush I hadn't experienced since becoming Lead Detective. I don't know what made it so different, maybe it was being in a different place or working with Storm again, but I was ready to dive in. I would have to let these thoughts go for now, though, because my transfer was still in limbo. No point in getting worked up if I wasn't able to officially help out.

In addition to my daily walks I had also been eating better. During my last appointment a month ago, Dr. Monroe, a beautiful black woman in her late fifties, scolded me for the twenty pounds I'd added to my once-toned frame.

"Stop eating like a teenager," she'd warned, "and pay attention to your food choices, or you'll be on meds for the rest of your life."

Trying to shake her voice out of my thoughts, I walked into my kitchen to make a smoothie and realized I was out of spinach. Making a fruit smoothie would have sufficed but I was trying to get more greens in lately. I decided to drive the ten minutes into town to this new bistro I'd discovered two days ago.

One of the things I loved about this island was that there was hardly any traffic, no matter the time of day. I pulled up to the yellow brick building and entered the shop. After placing my smoothie order, I leaned against the counter looking at the T.V. The newscaster was discussing the recent murders in the once quiet town and how everyone was in fear for their life.

Looks like you could have used my help, Special Agent Christophe, I thought sarcastically.

I had a special talent for seeing things in a different way which made me very successful in my line of work. Storm had suggested more than once that we write a training manual on investigating but I never had the time, until now.

My phone rang and my parents' home number appeared. I sighed, thinking it was probably my sister calling from their line. *Let me get this over with...*

"Hello?"

"Veronica," my mother said in a panicked voice and I immediately thought of my father.

"Ma, what's wrong...?" I said loudly, "Is it Dad?"

The other patrons looked my way and I lowered my voice. The guy behind the counter touched my shoulder, then handed me my smoothie. I grabbed it from him, mouthed thank you and walked toward the front door that was being held open for me. I looked at the man holding it and saw it was none other than Special Agent Christophe. Caught off guard I managed a curt nod to thank him, then continued walking to my vehicle. As I approached it I looked back and saw he was staring after me.

"Veronica, you there?" my mother was saying.

"Yes, sorry Ma, I'm here."

"I said, it's not your father," she stated. I exhaled and my heartbeat started to slow.

"Have you heard?" she asked.

"Heard what?"

"About Tanya Jameson."

"Tanya?" Tanya Jameson had been my elementary school best friend. I hadn't spoken to her in years. "What, is she about to get married?" I said in a sarcastic tone.

My mother sighed heavily. "Well she was engaged, but no, she won't be getting married. She is being charged with murder."

"What!" I said and placed my smoothie on the top of my car and leaned against the door. "Murder?"

"Yes, her mom called this morning, saying they arrested Tanya last night. She didn't know what to do but she remembered that you were a detective and wanted to know if you would help her."

"Help her with what?" I asked.

"Veronica… help her find out what's going on."

With a sigh, I grabbed my smoothie off the hood and got into the car. "Okay, Ma, I'll call and see what I can find out, but tell her not to get her hopes up. Detectives are pretty territorial about their crime investigations."

Just then I saw Special Agent Christophe exit the bistro, with a small white pastry bag and a coffee cup in his hand, he got into his vehicle. He was staring at me in the rearview mirror as he backed out of the parking space, then tilted his head to me and drove away. *The man is so strange*, I thought as his car disappeared around the corner.

"Veronica…" my mom said, once again bringing me back to the present.

"I'll let you know what I find."

"Okay… thank you, baby," she replied, then hung up the phone.

Tanya Jameson and I were best friends from kindergarten up to the fifth grade. From the time I saw her walk into the classroom, with her thick glasses and thick braids, I knew I wanted to be her friend. And not because she was the only other black girl in my class, but because she had a Fraggle Rock backpack. I loved that show. I invited her to my table, and from that moment on we were inseparable, trading our lunches and walking home together every day. I was sure we would be best friends for life, but at the beginning of fifth grade she started hanging with some new kids and getting into stuff like hanging out with boys, skipping school, and smoking cigarettes. I knew my parents would kill me if I did any of those things, so I refused to participate; that made me uncool and that was the end of our friendship. I would see Tanya around the neighborhood and at school, but we never talked or hung out again. After graduating high school Tanya went away to college in Saint Louis and I attended the local community college, but our parents still attended the same church, which was how Mom heard about the arrest.

I sat on my sofa, looking at the melting smoothie that I placed on the table thirty minutes earlier. The news about Tanya had taken away my appetite. She had been a big part of my childhood, and though we weren't friends anymore I wanted to help her in any way I could. On the other hand, did I really want to get involved? What if she had done what they were accusing her of? After all, I didn't know the person she had become. Already I could feel my shoulders tensing as the stress that had disappeared in the past several days returned. I sighed. If I didn't help and she was wrongly convicted, I would never be able to live with myself.

My decision made, I picked up my phone. The first call I made was to Storm. He had connections everywhere and was my best shot at getting information.

He answered on the second ring. "Hi Veronica, how are you holding up?"

"I've been better. Listen, Storm, I know you are busy with the case but I have a favor to ask."

"What do you need?" he said without hesitation, and I knew it was in part because he still felt guilty about not telling me about the murders. I told him what I knew about Tanya's case, which was very little – just her name and that she'd been arrested for murdering her lover. He said he would make a couple of calls and get back with me.

In the meantime, I decided to do a little research of my own. I opened my laptop and typed Tanya L Jameson into Google. A couple of news articles had been posted about her arrest but they didn't tell me anything I hadn't already heard from my mother. I then clicked on the Saint Louis Police Department website and, sure enough, there was Tanya's mugshot. She looked the same as she did in high school, pretty with flawless caramel-colored skin, but instead of her long curly hair she sported a short pixie cut that suited her slim face.

I moved on to Facebook and typed in Tanya's name. According to her profile she was single and there was no mention of Jonathan anywhere. I flipped through her photos, and aside from a couple of her parents the majority were from work events. Tanya appeared to be very active with her career. I kept scrolling then, came across a picture taken a month ago of her receiving an award. The nice-looking man standing behind her was staring at her in a way that suggested they were more than colleagues. I took a picture of the screen with my cell phone. The last picture I came across was captioned,

"Promotion – Brookes Brothers." Tanya stood in the center of the picture with five men surrounding her, including the man from the previous one. I took another screenshot.

I typed Brookes Brothers in the search engine and clicked on the link, searching for anything of interest. I clicked the Senior Staff tab and saw the CEO of Brookes Brothers and the other founding members. Then I came to Charles Brookes Jr., who I identified as the man staring at Tanya in the pictures. I wrote his name in my notepad. The picture of Tanya on their website didn't do her justice. She looked stiff and corporate, not like the vivacious girl I remembered.

I then remember my mother saying that the victim, Jonathan Skagel, worked with her and typed his name in the search box. A moment later I was starting at a very handsome man, and one well established in the company. Well, I could certainly see why Tanya was attracted to him. Then I googled him and immediately stopped when I saw a picture of him with a woman and two small kids. The photo was from Sylvia Skagel's blog page.

"He was married," I said out loud as I leaned back on the sofa. I started reading Sylvia's blog, which was very interesting, and lost track of time until my stomach started rumbling. I looked at the clock and saw it was a little past eight. No wonder I was hungry; I hadn't had anything all day except for a few sips of the smoothie which was still on the counter, completely melted.

I walked into the kitchen, opened the drawer and flipped through the stack of take-out menus Storm had left for me until I came across one for Thai food. I loved Thai food. I ordered Red Shrimp Curry with steamed rice and an order of spring rolls. The lady on the other end stated that my food wouldn't arrive for forty minutes. I was rummaging in the fridge for something to snack on when something dawned on me. Since my transfer hasn't gone through yet my password should still work for the Atlanta Police Database. I knew it was a long shot, but I wanted to see if Tanya had any priors in our database; after all, she had grown up around the area.

I logged into the database using my user id and password and hesitantly pressed the submit button. I was granted access, but my excitement soon turned to disappointment because this meant that my transfer was still pending. I started typing in Tanya's name when my phone rang. I immediately thought of Storm, then saw it was an unfamiliar number with an Atlanta area code. I hesitated, then picked up the phone.

"Hello?"

"Why are you roaming the database?"

I smiled as I recognized the voice of my former partner, Black. Detective Timothy Black and I had worked together for seven years. A former computer programmer turned detective, he was a short, attractive Latino man married to a Tyra Banks look alike. I'd always jokingly asked him what she saw in him, but I knew what she saw: Black was the most genuine and loving person I'd ever met. He and Natalie had been married for eight years and had a set of five-year-old twin boys. Black and I spoke the same lingo, we liked the same foods, he understood me, and I understood him; our partnership was perfect and I trusted him with my life. The shooting less than a month ago had taken a toll mentally on both of us. I had reacted to it by transferring out; he had applied for a desk job.

"Hey partner, it's good hearing your voice."

"Hey Veronica, what's up?" he said with a questioning tone.

"How do you know I signed on?"

"You remember that scare with the system a couple of weeks back?"

"Yeah…"

"Well, they put me in charge of the investigation."

"Wow, I guess you weren't kidding about not being in the field anymore."

"Yup. It hasn't been an easy transition for me but I've been enjoying getting home at a decent hour and Natalie loves that I'm not on the streets anymore. It's a nice change of pace."

"Okay, what have you done with my partner? I never thought I would hear you being okay with a desk job."

"Well, both of us are full of surprises," he stated with laughter in his voice. "What are you looking for? Maybe I can help."

"A former classmate of mine was arrested last night in a connection with the murder of her fiancé' and I promised my mom that I'd check it out."

"Oh wow. I figured it might be about those murders down there. What's going on? Is it a serial?"

"That's a long story I'd rather not get into right now… in the meantime I wanted to do some research on my childhood friend, make sure she doesn't have any priors in our system."

"Veronica, we can get in big trouble for this, since you are technically on leave."

"I know, I will be quick," I said with a pleading tone.

Black let out a heavy sigh. "Okay Veronica, but make it real quick. How is Storm?"

"He's Storm," I said.

We chatted for a couple more minutes, then promised to catch up again soon. As soon as we ended the call I got back to work, knowing I had only a few minutes before Black shut me out. If Captain Morgan found out I was logged in, Black and I could be in serious trouble.

The doorbell rang and I quickly paid and tipped the delivery person and headed back to my research. I found no priors for Tanya, then just to be thorough I typed in

Jonathan Skagel's name. Nothing for him either. I had worked all day and was still at ground zero.

CHAPTER 11

TANYA L. JAMESON

The smell of bacon woke me up. Normally that would be enough to get me up but after a night of tossing and turning I just wanted to stay in bed all day. Out of habit I reached over and grabbed my phone – not that I wanted to look at it. I certainly wasn't going to check out social media, not with my arrest in the news and that video from my neighbor floating around. I did see that I had three missed calls and several messages, most of them from Ginger and Charles. I played the first voice message and heard Charles' distraught voice. "Tanya, give me a call, I am in your corner, whatever you need." I started to dial his number but then heard a light tap at my door.

"Yes?"

My dad opened the door. "Good morning, babygirl, are you hungry? Your mom cooked a big breakfast for you."

"I'm not hungry, but I know Mom's not going to take no for an answer."

"You're right about that," Dad chuckled. "I'll let her know you'll be down in a few."

As soon as he closed the door behind him I got out of the bed and looked in the mirror. I looked horrible – my eyes were red and baggy from all the crying and my hair was a mess. I went to the bathroom to fix myself up a bit. As I was brushing my teeth my phone rang; it was a number I didn't recognize. I rinsed my mouth and stared at my phone for a moment before hitting the green button.

"Hello?" I said softly.

"Tanya?" a familiar voice came across the line.

"Oh my gosh, Veronica?" It came out as a question, though I knew without a doubt who it was.

"Yes, its Veronica," she said, "Your mom gave me your number."

"Oh wow, it's good to hear your voice." My face fell when I realized why she was calling. "Please don't tell me I'm in the news all the way in Atlanta!"

"No, your mom called," Veronica said.

"My mom called... why?"

"She asked me to help you."

"Help me...?"

"Yes, since I am a detective she thought you could use my help."

"But why would I need your help, I didn't kill anybody!"

"I guess that's what she wants me to help clear up."

"Veronica, I am so sorry she called you, but I don't need help. I spent one night in jail, this all is a misunderstanding that will soon go away. I wish this call was under different circumstances and that we could catch up, but I can't right now."

"I see. Well, take care of yourself."

"You too."

I was furious at my mother. Bad enough everyone at her church knew about my situation because the deacon had helped get me out – now she was going around asking for help from childhood friends? Hadn't I been embarrassed enough? I walked down the stairs ready to confront her, but then I saw the deacon sitting at the table eating with my parents.

"We tried to wait on you, honey, but no one wants to eat cold eggs." My mother put a forkful of eggs in her mouth. She had cooked a feast and judging from the heap of food on his plate the deacon sure was enjoying it.

I walked into the kitchen, grabbed a plate off the counter and scooped some lukewarm scrambled eggs onto it, along with two strips of bacon. The seat across from the deacon was free and I settled myself into it.

"How are you holding up?" he asked.

I looked at him. "As expected."

"Well I was thinking that we could start going over your whereabouts the past week."

I stared at him.

"After breakfast, of course." He smiled.

My eyes never left him. "Why? I didn't kill Jonathan."

"I know, but as I told you we have to build our defense in case this thing goes to court."

"Court?" I said and stood up from the table, "I am not going to court!"

My mom grabbed my hand. "Honey, Deacon Mosley is here to help, and though he's a dear friend we are paying him for his expertise."

"By the hour... plus expenses!" my dad blurted out. Mom gave him a curt look then continued. "He is here to help you, and he is an expert in criminal cases."

"Criminal? I am not a criminal!"

"We know you're not, but you are a person of interest in a murder investigation." Her eyes pleaded with me. "Deacon was going on vacation when I called, and he came, so please let him help."

"Tanya," Deacon Mosley said gently, "the quicker we can produce an alibi, the quicker this can go away."

"Okay." My eyes welled with tears again.

"Can anyone confirm your whereabouts on the Saturday morning that Jonathan was murdered?" the Deacon questioned.

I winced at the word *murdered* and shook my head no.

"You said you went jogging, did you speak to anyone? Did you stop to get a coffee? Anything that someone can confirm?"

I shook my head again. "No one saw me. I went for a quick jog then I came back home, by myself. I was upset with Jonathan."

"Okay, this is just going to take longer than expected. They have evidence."

"What do you mean, evidence? What evidence?" I said, looking between my mother and my father.

"Apparently a piece of jewelry was found in the park not too far from where Jonathan's car was discovered. It has your name engraved on it."

I looked baffled and wondered why he was just now telling me this. The only piece of jewelry I had with my name engraved was the watch my dad gave to me when I finished grad school. I quickly raced up the stairs to check my jewelry box; it was gone. I looked around my entire room, throwing clothes out of the drawer, but it wasn't there. I was extra careful with my watch; it meant a lot to me. I always kept it in my jewelry box.

Slowly walking down the stairs, I heard the Deacon say, "We need to hire someone."

"Hire someone? Like who?"

"I am a lawyer, not an Investigator. We need someone to dig up evidence to prove you're innocent, or that someone else is guilty. The DA has been under a lot of heat lately and they need to pin this murder on someone. Right now that someone is you."

I sat on the sofa and put my head in my lap. "This can't be happening," I mumbled.

"I can call someone… a detective friend of mine, he can help," the Deacon stated. "Tanya?"

"No, I have someone," I said vaguely. Deacon Mosley gave me a surprised look, then handed me his card. "Give them my number, we need to get on this ASAP." He stood from the table and buttoned his suit jacket. "I will head back to the hotel and get to work." Then he grabbed his briefcase, told me he would be in touch, and headed out the door. My parents followed him outside, probably to find out what he thought my chances of beating this were. Great. No doubt my neighbors were glued to their windows, watching to see what was going on. I pulled out my phone and pressed the last number received. I hoped Veronica was still willing to help me.

CHAPTER 12

VERONICA REDMOND

I had to admit I was relieved when Tanya turned down my offer to help; I had too much on my plate already. But my relief was short-lived because not less than an hour after I hung up with her she called back saying she had changed her mind. I told her that I would be on the first flight out.

After we hung up, I went online and fortunately found a flight that was leaving in ninety minutes. Then I called for a taxi, dragged out the suitcase I had unpacked less than a week earlier, and began throwing clothes and toiletries into it. I had just finished zipping it up when I heard the honking of the taxi driver outside. I sighed as I slid into the backseat; I could have used another week of relaxing but there was nothing I could do about that now.

On my way to the airport, I went down a mental checklist. I had already talked to Storm before calling Tanya and he was okay with me leaving just as long as I came back once my paperwork was completed. I pulled out my phone and called Tanya's lawyer, David Mosley, who had offered to pick me up at the airport. "Looks like we have our work cut out for us," he said, stating the obvious. "See you when you get here." I hung up the phone and begin thinking about questions to ask Tanya. She would have to be totally honest if I was going to help her.

I made it through TSA and to my gate within thirty minutes, just before they started boarding. The flight was just under two hours, which gave me plenty of time to go over what I knew again and write down the questions I wanted to ask Tanya. I boarded the plane and made my way to my seat, where I was sandwiched between a teenaged boy with headphones on and an older black gentleman who graciously offered to help me with my carry-on.

So, chivalry is not dead, I thought as he placed my bag in the overhead storage bin. I took out my notepad and immediately begin jotting down questions: *When did you meet Jonathan? What was the nature of your relationship with him? How much of your personal life did he know? Who at the office knew about your relationship? Who are your friends? What church do you go to? When was the last time you and Jonathan had sex?*

I felt the man next to me looking at my paper and glanced up at him. *Chivalrous and nosy,* I thought, glad that he looked away without asking any questions. I needed this time to focus.

As soon as the plane landed I called David Mosley, who said he would be at the airport in fifteen minutes. I exited the doors of the Saint Louis airport and immediately spotted the red SUV he'd described. There was a short, balding man standing outside of it, looking at me curiously. I waved to let him know who I was and began walking briskly in his direction.

"Hello Detective, David Mosley," he said formally, hand outstretched, then opened the passenger door for me. "Veronica is fine", I slid inside while he loaded my luggage into the SUV. *Two chivalrous men in one day*, I thought, smiling to myself.

As he slipped into the driver's seat I said, "You don't seem like the 'red car' type of guy."

He looked at me and smiled. "It's Mr. Jameson's. He's allowing me to drive it while I am here."

I nodded.

"How was your flight?" he asked.

"It was productive," I pulled the legal pad from the side of my purse and read him my questions.

He smiled again. "I see you're diving right in. I'd read that about you."

So he'd done some research on me, I thought. I almost mentioned that I had googled him as well, but remained silent.

"I was able to reserve you a suite on the same floor of the hotel as me. There's a small meeting room in between that we can use as our workspace, I hope that is okay..."

"Yes, that's perfect," I said, then turned to look out the window, trying to get a feel for the city.

The rest of the car ride was silent, with each of us lost in our own thoughts. After about twenty minutes he pulled into the parking lot of the Four Seasons Hotel.

I glanced at him, eyebrow raised. Clearly the Jamesons had spared no expense in hiring their daughter an attorney.

I also noticed that Mosely was a man who was used to the finer things in life. I could tell by the way he spoke to the valet – courteous but with authority.

The hotel was very beautiful, overlooking the well-known Saint Louis Arch. As we walked into the lobby another uniformed valet came to collect my luggage. David gave him my room number, then turned and handed me my key.

"May I show you to your room?" he asked.

"Of course," I said, following him to the elevators. When we got in David swiped his card over a metal plate and then pressed the tenth floor.

"You will need your key to access our floor, so make sure you have it on you at all times."

"Okay thanks," I replied, thinking again about how much these fancy digs were costing Tanya's parents.

"You're in Room 1011," David said when the elevator doors opened. "I'm in 1015 and the meeting room is 1013. I have some things to attend to and you probably want to get settled. Shall we meet for dinner at, say, six o'clock? The restaurant downstairs has the best salt and pepper lobster."

I glanced at my watch and saw it was just after three. "Sure, that sounds great."

David nodded, then walked two doors down to his room. I swiped the key on my door and walked in to see a beautiful room with stunning views. I was about to walk out onto the balcony when there was a knock on my door. I glanced through the peephole and saw the bellman holding my luggage.

I could get used to this, I thought.

Once he was gone I called Storm and my parents to let them know I had made it, then I took a quick shower and laid across the bed for a power nap. At 5:55, feeling refreshed and famished, I slipped into the elevator.

I was crossing the lobby of the hotel when I heard a female voice say my name. Startled, I turned around and saw Tanya walking quickly toward me. She greeted me with a hug, and over her shoulder I could see her parents walking up behind her. Though I was happy to see them, I was slightly annoyed. I had been looking forward to catching up on the case with David without any distractions.

"Oh Veronica, thank you so much for coming. You haven't changed a bit," Mrs. Jameson said as she gave me a hug. Mr. Jameson reached and touched my hand and gave it a gentle squeeze.

"It's nice seeing you all," I replied warmly, "It's been too long."

Just then David Mosley joined us. "I see that everyone is here, why don't we head in."

When we entered the restaurant, the hostess immediately guided us to a special table in the back. As soon as we sat down Tanya suggested that we didn't talk about the case and just enjoy dinner. Despite my frustration I decided to just go with the flow. It would allow Tanya to relax so I could get a good idea of the person she had become.

We had a couple of stares our way, and I figured people recognized Tanya from the news, but other than that we had a very pleasant evening. Dinner was great, and we had plenty of laughs reminiscing about our childhood days. After we said our goodbyes, I proceeded to the elevator while the Deacon stayed in the lobby talking church with Tanya's parents.

I stepped onto the elevator and turned around to see Tanya coming in behind me.

"Oh, I thought you were with the others." The elevator closed, and I swiped my keycard across the black metal plate then pressed the tenth-floor button.

"Sorry, but I need to talk to you one on one," she said.

"Can this wait until tomorrow? It's getting late…" I looked at the numbers light up as we passed each floor – four, five, six…

"I need to get this off my chest right now," Tanya said.

Ten… the elevator opened and we stepped out. "Okay," I said, "What is it?"

She looked at me. "Not out here in the open. I'd rather the Deacon not know I am here."

I hesitated, not because I was afraid or intimated by Tanya; she had no reason to harm me and if she tried I could take her down in two seconds flat. I just hoped she wasn't trying to take another trip down memory lane. Then again, I was curious to hear what she had to say.

"Okay," I sighed and walked to my room, with Tanya quick on my heels. She headed straight for the minibar.

"Help yourself," I said curtly as I threw my purse on the bed then walked over to the recliner and sat down.

I watched Tanya pour herself a shot of tequila and swallow it in one gulp. Someone knocked on the door and we looked at it, then each other, like we were kids who'd just gotten caught doing something they weren't supposed to do. Tanya quickly slipped into the bathroom while I went to the door and looked through the peephole.

"Mr. Mosley," I said as I opened the door. I hated that Tanya had me feeling like I am doing something wrong.

He waved his hand. "Oh, call me David or Deacon."

"Okay, David it is," I smiled, then moved aside so he could enter.

"I was wondering if you had time now to get together, I could update you on what I know, and we can plan our next course of action. I told the Jamesons that we would be over to Tanya's house around nine a.m. with some ideas for a defense."

"Actually, I'm really beat and not at my best. Can we meet in the meeting room at seven a.m.? "

He nodded. "That'll be fine."

I opened the door, hoping that David would get the hint, but he glanced around the room, his eyes stopping at the mini bar with the opened bottle of tequila and the empty shot glass.

"Get some rest, Veronica, we have a long day ahead of us tomorrow," he said, then walked out the door.

"Will do…"

A moment later Tanya walked out of the bathroom. "Whew, that was close…"

"Tanya, what do you want? I don't keep secrets from my partners, and while I am here David is my partner."

Tanya walked to the window and peered out. She was beginning to irritate me with this secrecy thing. I went to the minibar and poured myself a shot of tequila and downed it.

Tanya turned to me. "I talked to Jonathan."

"What do you mean you talked to Jonathan?" I blurted out, almost choking on my drink.

She sat in the chair by the window. "That day... the day he was killed."

My eyes widened. "David said that you hadn't seen or spoken to him in weeks."

"I know. I was scared, Veronica. I didn't kill him, I just wanted..." She glared back towards the window. "I wanted answers, I wanted to confront him, to curse him out..."

I poured another shot of tequila and downed it, and was surprised when my head immediately started to pound. *Wow, I must be even more exhausted than I thought.* Liquor never hit me this hard or this fast. I couldn't even think straight.

"Tanya, I am not feeling so good," I said, sitting down on the bed. "You have to go, we will talk about this tomorrow."

Tanya looked as though she was about to argue, then she just grabbed her bag and silently exited my room.

~   ~   ~

My eyes squinted as the sun pierced through the window. I jumped from the bed, and glanced at the clock on the nightstand: 6:22 a.m. I sighed in relief; it would be very unprofessional if I was late to my first meeting with David. My head was still hurting and I felt slightly nauseous. I didn't think I was such a lightweight; I'd only had a glass of wine at dinner and then the two shots of tequila. I went into the bathroom, hoping a hot shower would sober me up.

A few minutes later I felt like a new woman as I pawed through my suitcase for something to wear. *I'm sure David would be overdressed,* I thought as I pulled a plain grey blouse over my head. In my line of work, I was more concerned with being clean and comfortable rather than stylish.

While in the shower, I'd decided to tell David what Tanya told me. I was not here to rekindle a friendship, I was here to stop Tanya from going to jail for something she didn't do. Then again, I wasn't totally convinced of her innocence, especially after last night's confession. I'd seen more than my fair share of 'crimes of passion' by schoolteachers and soccer moms and I was not about to keep her secrets. If she asked me to leave because I shared imperative information with my partner, then so be it.

With five minutes left before our meeting, I quickly finished pulling my curls into a high bun, ran lip gloss over my lips, and gathered my notepad and pen. When I opened the door to the adjoining conference room David was already there, sipping on a cup of coffee and eating what looked to be a croissant. He had papers spread across the table.

"Good morning, David," I said as I entered the room.

"Good morning Veronica, did you sleep well?"

"Yes, I did, thank you."

"The beds here are amazing, aren't they? I have one like it at home." David pointed to his back. "It has helped me tremendously. By the way, I took the liberty of ordering us breakfast." David gestured toward a room service cart with fresh coffee, juice, an assortment of pastries, and a variety of fruit.

I poured myself a cup of black coffee and put a croissant on a plate. I then took a seat at the table, suddenly nervous about telling him what Tanya had revealed last night.

"Let me fill you in on the case while you eat," David began.

"Before you do, I need to let you know something…"

"Okay."

I didn't respond right away and he raised an eyebrow at me.

"What is it, Veronica," he prompted.

"Last night, after dinner, Tanya came to my room."

He took his glasses off and shifted forward.

"She informed me that she talked to Jonathan…… the morning he was murdered."

David was now visibly flustered. "What else did she say?" he questioned with a calm tone that didn't match his demeanor.

"That was all. I stopped her and asked her to leave, I wanted you to be there if she was going to reveal more." I sighed and leaned back in my chair.

"Thank you for doing that. I specifically asked Tanya when she'd last spoken to Jonathan and she told me two weeks ago. If she's keeping information from me I cannot and will not help her. I have to be able to trust my clients." David stood and began to pace the floor.

"I agree. Transparency's a must, that's why I decided to tell you."

David stopped pacing and turned towards me. "Why wouldn't you tell me this?"

My eyes shifted.

"Did Tanya ask you to withhold this information from me?"

Crap. I took a sip of coffee to avoid answering his question.

"I see," David said. He put on his glasses and grabbed his phone off the table. "I have to make a call, but please familiarize yourself with the case." He pointed to the papers spread across the table. I could hear the phone ringing on the other end of David's cell phone as he exited the meeting room.

The first set of papers on the table were Jonathan's autopsy report. I was surprised that David had this since

Tanya hadn't yet been officially charged with the murder. David must have connections in high places.

The autopsy showed that Jonathan was killed with a single bullet to the chest at close range with a nine-millimeter. It had happened in a rental car, in a secluded part of Forest Hill Park. He must have been meeting someone and the meeting didn't go as expected. A watch with Tanya's name engraved on it was found in the park near the crime scene.

That's an odd coincidence, I thought to myself, *but since Tanya lied about talking to Jonathan she could also be lying about actually seeing him that day*

I flipped through the other papers to see that Jonathan was in debt up to his eyeballs. The next set of papers caught my attention. The day before his death, Jonathan was put on suspension without pay from Brookes Brothers with a pending investigation for potential embezzlement. A moment later I was startled by David returning to the room.

"You're jumpy for a detective," he noted.

"Is everything okay?" I asked, ignoring his comment. "It wasn't my intention to bring any tension to this case." I took a sip of coffee.

"Everything is okay now, and it's not your fault. Tanya withheld pertinent information from me, and no lawyer wants to be blindsided by their own client."

I nodded.

"We have an understanding now." He reached for his cup of coffee, realized it was cold and set it back down. "Now, what can I fill in for you?"

CHAPTER 13

TANYA L. JAMESON

My phone chirped, indicating a text message. I looked at the time and groaned: 7:00 a.m. Ever since the police showed up at my door and arrested me, I hadn't been getting much sleep, I was awakened by the slightest noise. The text message was from Charles: Hope you are okay.

I sat up in my bed and dialed his cell number. He answered on the first ring.

"Tanya! How are you?"

"Well," I replied, "I was asleep until a message came in… Why are you up so early?"

"Sorry to wake you," he said. "Actually it's late for me – I'm headed into work."

"My gosh, so much has been going on I can't even keep track of the days of the week."

"I can't imagine." Charles went silent then; most likely he was searching for something to say, but what? I knew he must still be reeling from the fact that I was seeing Jonathan, let alone arrested for his murder.

"Charles, I know there are a lot of things you want to know and there are things that I want to tell you, but I can't right now," I said.

"Tanya, I am not asking for an explanation; you don't owe me anything. I just wanted you to know that I am here for you."

"Thank you, that means a lot. What about my job... will I still have one after all of this?"

"Tanya, you are the best accountant I know. I'll hire a temp to do the basics and I'll handle the big stuff, so you just worry about clearing your name. Your job will be here."

I sighed heavily. At least that was one thing I didn't have to worry about. I was about to thank him again when my phone beeped with another call. I looked at it and saw David Mosely's number. I grunted in frustration.

I was over all of this. Yes, I had been arrested, and maybe I was still a person of interest in Jonathan's murder, but honestly, I felt like all of this was for nothing. If the police had something on me, they would have charged me already. If it wasn't for the Deacon promising the District Attorney that I would stay in town, I would be on a plane to Jamaica forgetting all about this. Instead, I was a prisoner in my own house, hiding from nosy neighbors. I just wanted this all to go away and it wouldn't as long as the Deacon and Veronica were around. Maybe I'd made a mistake in asking her to come.

"Charles, I will have to call you later. It's my lawyer."

"Okay, take care Tanya, I'm here for you," Charles said, then hung up the phone.

~ ~ ~

"Good morning, Deacon," I said, "I thought we were meeting at nine…?"

"We are, Tanya, but I need to clarify something with you. Do you have a few minutes?" He sounded upset, maybe a little angry.

"Sure."

"Tanya, I took your case as a favor to your parents because they are longtime friends of mine. I respect them and they respect me. I decided to forego my much-needed vacation to come here to help you. My wife has been looking forward to our vacation for an entire year and because she loves your parents and YOU, she agreed to postpone."

I stayed silent, knowing better than to interrupt him.

"At this point I don't know if I can trust you, and I need to be able to trust my clients."

So that's what this was about. "I guess Veronica told you what I told her last night."

"Yes, she did. Tanya, you lied to me; you lied about something that could send you to prison for a very long time. I can't help you like this; I *won't* help you like this." His tone was deadly serious.

"I'm sorry Deacon," I said quietly, "but– "

"Tanya, now is not the time for excuses. I don't care about excuses, I don't care how you think it will look, or if you think this bit of information wasn't important. I need to know everything and when I ask a question, I need the TRUTH. If that is too much to ask, let me know now!"

I felt like a ten-year-old schoolgirl being scolded for lying to her teacher, but I understood.

"You're right, Deacon, and I appreciate you being here. I promise… no more lies, I will be open and honest with you from this point forward."

"Excellent, so we will see you at nine then?" he asked.

"Yes, I will be here, ready to answer any questions you have… honestly."

With that, the deacon hung up. I laid the phone down and crawled back under the covers, tears welling in my eyes. Though I didn't want to believe this was happening, it was, and I needed to take it more seriously. The quicker the Deacon and Veronica could clear my name, the quicker I could move on with my life. I hadn't even had the time to mourn Jonathan.

CHAPTER 14

SYLVIA S. SKAGEL

I didn't know which part was more disheartening – the fact that my kids would grow up without a father or my kids finding out that their father was taken from them by his mistress. Sophia was smart, and I was sure she had already read some of the articles on the internet related to his death. The only reason this made the news was because Jonathan was employed by Brookes Brothers, one of the top law firms in the country. A top executive killed by another? Talk about a scandal. The press was having a field day trying to tarnish the firm's reputation.

I'd never heard of Tanya L. Jameson, the "person of interest," before, but I could guess who she was: Jonathan's latest conquest. She was not his usual type;

Jonathan used to go for them much younger and naïve, but the pictures I saw depicted a confident woman in her mid to late thirties, one that appeared too smart to fall for his antics. I wondered if she knew that the day before his death he'd been suspended on suspicion of embezzlement. Maybe she was the type that acted strong in public but was weak and insecure behind closed doors.

Jonathan had told me about the suspension, and that he was staying in Saint Louis for a couple of more days to get to the bottom of things. Now come to find out this Tanya person worked out of the Saint Louis office! I tried not to think about all the business trips he had been taking there lately. And if he had been embezzling money it would be nice to know where that money was because I could use it right now. To find out that your husband has been murdered was bad enough; to find out that you were basically broke with two kids to raise was too much to handle. I learned how bad things were from Kevin, Jonathan's assistance. Kevin, a nice young man around twenty-five, had come by the house to offer his condolences and his assistance with the funeral. He considered Jonathan a mentor and Jonathan had trusted him with everything, so God only knew what secrets he held.

Kevin sat across the table from me as I went over the arrangements I had in mind.

"Here is our life insurance policy," I said. "Can you do whatever needs to be done to get this taken care of? I would like to bury Jonathan as soon they release his body."

Kevin took the policy out of my hand and typed something into his computer.

"I'm sorry to tell you this Mrs. Skagel but this policy has lapsed."

"What, what do you mean lapsed? This is a million-dollar policy."

"Yes ma'am, I know, about six months ago Jonathan told me to stop making payments on it, to use the money for other bills. I told him that the policy would lapse, and he told me he would take care of it. When I heard he was… um of his death, I checked into the policy and learned he had never made the payments. I just checked this policy number with the one I had on file to ensure that it wasn't a different one, but it's the same and it has expired."

I fought against the tears welling up in my eyes.

Kevin continued, "I am sorry, Mrs. Skagel, but I do need to tell you that your other bills are behind as well."

I glanced up at him.

"What do you mean, what other bills?"

"I am sorry," he repeated.

"Please stop saying you are sorry for things you didn't do," I snapped.

"Yes, ma'am, I just hate to be the one to tell you all of this... Your house, your cars, your utilities, everything is past due. I have been shuffling these bills for the last six months, putting just the minimum on each and sometimes asking for extensions, just to keep the creditors at bay."

I rubbed my temples, unable to believe this was happening. I had trusted Jonathan with all the finances, and now my life had turned into a Lifetime movie.

"I can't believe this is happening," I repeated aloud. "So, you have access to our checking and savings accounts?"

"Yes ma'am."

"How much is in there?"

"A little over twenty-seven thousand," Kevin said and lowered his head.

I was incredulous. "And that includes savings?"

"Yes ma'am."

"But he was making over three hundred thousand a year at Brookes Brothers, plus bonuses! Where did it all go?"

"I don't know," Kevin said.

"What you mean you don't know?"

"He would make withdrawals but I had no idea what he did with that money..."

I knew it was unfair to expect Kevin to know the inner workings of my husband's devious mind – especially since I was unable to do so. I thanked the young man for coming by and let him know that I would be in touch.

What was I going to do? No insurance policy, the benefits from his job were still pending since he was on suspension without pay at the time of his death. I had taken out a policy on Jonathan a couple of years ago, it wasn't much, just seventy-five thousand, but it was enough to give me time to think about what I was going to do with my life. Unfortunately it would not pay out until the investigation was closed. I had about a hundred and thirty-eight thousand stashed away in my private bank account, thank God; otherwise I don't know what I would have done. I could only hope and pray that between that and the twenty-seven thousand in the bank account I could pay off our bills and have enough for me and the kids to live off for a while. The first step was to figure out exactly how much we owed.

CHAPTER 15

SYLVIA S. SKAGEL

Four days after my husband's murder I decided to proceed with the funeral arrangements. His body hasn't been released but I didn't need the body to have a ceremony. Looking at a dead body in a casket had always given me the creeps anyway, so instead of the traditional funeral I planned a very small ceremony with a few close family members and friends. It was pleasant enough. I gave instructions to the hospital on where to send the body when it was released and instructions to the funeral director. Kevin was a huge help; he not only helped me to stay under budget for the funeral, he also put me in contact with a top-notch realtor who would stage the house and put it on the market. The realtor informed me that I should be able to get above market, given the size of the home and the community we live in. At least something was going in my favor.

My parents had been wonderful, watching the kids for me while I figured all this out. It was a huge relief not to have to leave them with strangers when their lives were already being turned upside down. Telling them about the impending move and that they'd have to change schools would be hard. At least Jonathan was current on their tuition, but I wouldn't be able to keep that up for long. Ever since Jonathan's death I'd felt like I had been holding my breath, waiting for the next awful blow. Life wasn't the best with Jonathan, but I believed him when he said that everything would be alright. Now it would be up to me to make that happen, for me and my children.

Kevin helped me to create a spreadsheet to figure out my finances, which was what I was currently working on. I saw why Jonathan trusted him; Kevin was a smart young man. I looked at the vibrating phone that laid beside my laptop and questioned if I wanted to answer it. It was my mother, and I knew why she was calling, I decided not to answer.

Yesterday morning Sophia had called, begging me to come and get them. She said she missed being home, and it was no wonder why. Six days with my mother was more than anyone could handle. I pulled into my parent's driveway a little after 7 p.m. Sophia and Jonathan Jr. rushed out of the house with their backpacks on. They must have really been homesick. They loved spending time with their grandparents but had never been at their house for more than a weekend. I was also sure they had plenty of questions about their father and what life would be like now.

My parents came to the door and waved. I didn't get out of the car, just waved back and said thank you. I wasn't ready for the conversation I needed to have with them about the financial situation Jonathan had left me in. But after the kids were settled in at home I decided to bite the bullet. I called my dad and spoke with him privately about the overdue bills and my plans to sell the house and pull the kids from private school. I knew he would tell my mother as soon as we got off the phone, then God help me.

~ ~ ~

It was Friday and I woke up early thinking the kids would be up and hungry, but they weren't. The house was eerily quiet for a Friday morning. I opened the door to Jonathan Jr.'s room and got worried when I didn't see him in his bed. The covers were pulled back and the light to his bathroom was off. That was weird. I opened the door to Sophia's room and saw her sleeping quietly with her brother snuggled right beside her. They looked so peaceful. I closed the door to allow them to sleep, then walked downstairs to make a cup of coffee.

The phone chirped, letting me know that I had a voicemail. I frowned, it was from my mother; she never left a voicemail unless she was really upset with me or really concerned about something. I sat at the table sipping my coffee and reviewing the spreadsheet Kevin had prepared. I closed the spreadsheet and pulled up the townhome listing Kevin emailed to me. Although my kids may not be in the same house, they could possibly still have the same friends close by. I really did not want to move in with my parents. The only person I told about the move was my yoga friend, Susan. She offered one of her bedrooms to me, but me and two kids, living in a two-bedroom apartment, with a person my kids didn't know, wouldn't work.

My parents, Roderick and Diane Sykes, never liked Jonathan. They saw him as conniving, manipulative and controlling, but I was having none of it. I was smitten, and Jonathan was the escape I needed to get out of their house.

After graduating from high school at seventeen, I went to the local university for one semester. It wasn't for me. My father told me that if I wanted to live under his roof, I had to be doing something productive with my life. So, after a little research, I enrolled in a dental assistant program at the local technical college. The program only took twelve months to complete, rather than the four years to get a degree, so I was up for trying it. Once in the program, I found myself actually liking it. I liked my classmates, my teacher, and the coursework. A month after my nineteenth birthday, I graduated from the program and got my first job at Performance Dental, a private practice owned by Dr. Claire Henderson. She was a young black oral surgeon who came to our class to speak about her practice and what it took to build our careers from the ground up. I was so intrigued by her knowledge and how passionate she was. I didn't know if I was interested in becoming an oral surgeon, which would have meant over a decade of schooling, but she made me feel like I could do anything I put my mind to. After her presentation, I nervously walked up to her and asked her questions about her practice. She gladly spoke to me and then handed me her business card. She told me that when I graduated from this program to give her a call and I did just that. She gave me my first job as a dental assistant. I started off making $9.50 an hour. I was excited about that, being that the minimum wage at that time was only $4.25. I was ready to get out of my parents' house, so I saved every penny I earned.

While at work one Tuesday afternoon, a tall, dark and handsome black man by the name of Jonathan Skagel walked into the office to have his wisdom teeth removed. I was immediately smitten with this charming guy. He talked so professionally, nothing like the guys in my neighborhood. While I was in the room gathering the instruments needed for his procedure, we made small talk. When the doctor came in to sedate him, this confident, strong guy became an intimidated scary mess. I was used to people's fear of the dentist but his was on another level. As the doctor eased the needle into his gums, he grabbed my arm and squeezed it so tight I almost punched him. Tears began to roll down his eyes, and I felt sorry for him, but he was hurting me. When the doctor removed the needle, he released his grip on my arm and I jerked away quickly and started rubbing it. After the procedure the dentist informed Jonathan of what he *would experience over the next couple of days and what he should do, then she left the room. After removing the chest cover from Jonathan, I asked if he had any questions, he nodded yes. He pointed to his mouth and made a writing motion with his hand. I handed him a notepad and pen from the adjacent table. He took it from me and begin scribbling on the pad. It read, "I'm sorry about your arm… let me make it up to you. Will you have dinner with me?" A smile formed on my face because I'd never met anyone like him before. I scribbled "yes" on the notepad, followed by my phone number, and handed it back to him. He read it and gave a gentle smile, then placed the piece of paper in his back pocket. The guys I usually dated around my neighborhood were guys that hustled for a living. They did what they needed to do to survive and made no apologies for it. But Jonathan was different, and from the looks of his tailored gray suit and tie, probably had a job in corporate America. I was very captivated by him.*

Jonathan called the next night and we talked on the phone for about thirty minutes, until his mouth started to hurt again. Before we hung up we confirmed our dinner plans for that Friday night. He told me to wear something fancy, so I went to the mall with my best friend, Sasha. I spent one hundred dollars on what the lady in Macy's called a cocktail dress and twenty-five dollars on a new pair of pumps. That night, I took extra care with my makeup and hair, pulling it up in a clip and allowing the curls to dangle in the front. I felt so grown up. My nosey little brother was at a friend's house and my parents went to an all-night prayer meeting at Grace Temple Church of God in Christ, so I knew they wouldn't be home until sometime after midnight. Jonathan had said he would pick up a little after six, plenty of time to make our seven o'clock reservations. I had never been to a restaurant where reservations were required, and I never dated someone with their own car before.

A sliver Toyota Camry pulled in the driveway and I waited for the horn to blow, letting me know he was waiting, but he didn't blow the horn. He got out of the car, walked to my door and knocked. I opened the door and his mouth literally dropped open.

"Wow, you look amazing."

"You look nice yourself," I said shyly.

This man wasn't just nice; he was FINE. He wore a baby blue button-down shirt with tan slacks and a sports jacket. He grabbed the shawl that I borrowed from my mother's closet out of my hand and draped it over my shoulders, then asked if I was ready to go. The answer was most definitely yes.

Jonathan took me to a very nice restaurant, Magnolia's Steakhouse, at the top of a fancy hotel. The views were amazing; I had never seen Chicago look so beautiful. I was very impressed but tried to act like I wasn't.

*"Don't be acting like you never been anywhere fancy,"
Sasha had advised, "You've watched enough T.V. to know how to act and what to order."*

I remembered someone from one of those cooking shows saying that when in doubt order the seafood or the special. The waiter came with menus and told us the specials, which I forgot as soon as he walked away. My eyes were everywhere in this restaurant, from the beautiful chandelier in the foyer to the dresses some of the women had on. I was happy that I'd decided to spend the extra money on this dress, I fit right in.

As I glanced over the menu, I saw a couple of seafood dishes and was relieved. I decided to go with the Cedar Plank Salmon and Jonathan thought that was a great choice and ordered it as well. The waiter offered several wine choices to go with our meal. I looked at Jonathan because I was only nineteen. He smiled, then ordered the bottle of pinot noir that the waiter suggested. We ate, laughed and drank for nearly two hours at this restaurant. After sharing the flaming dessert prepared right at our table, Jonathan paid the bill and we went for a drive downtown just admiring Chicago at night. Before I knew it, Jonathan was headed for my house. This had been the best night of my life and I didn't want it to end. I felt so special. We arrived at my house around ten, and knowing my parents wouldn't be home for another two hours, I asked if he wanted to come inside. He said yes.

Jonathan and I made love that night. It just felt right; everything about that night felt right. When the next day went by without a call from Jonathan, I was afraid that I would never see him again. But right before bed he called and asked if I wanted to go to a basketball game the next day. I said yes, and from there we were inseparable. After two months of dating, I brought him home to meet my parents. My dad took one look at him and told me that if I married him, I would be in for a lifetime of trouble. I ignored him; Jonathan was the best guy I had ever dated, and he treated me like a queen. I continued to see him despite my parents' disapproval, and three years later, we got married at the courthouse with my best friend Sasha and his best friend Julian as our witnesses. I was just twenty-two and he was twenty-six.

Four months into our marriage I saw what my father had seen. Jonathan demanded I quit my job, which I absolutely loved. He said I needed to learn how to be the wife that a man like him could be proud of and I couldn't be that by working. Jonathan also started an exercise schedule for me. He was very athletic and exercised every day, but I hated to sweat. Besides, I'd never understood the point since I never had much of a weight problem. But Jonathan said I looked frail and needed to build muscle. At first, I didn't think of his behavior as controlling; I just saw it as him wanting me to look good and to be healthy. So I took on the challenge of exercising four times a week and found I really liked it. I liked how my body transformed before my very eyes, I felt sexy, confident and I had abs.

I didn't know there was a problem until one day my brother called me and told me that Mom had been admitted to the hospital after being sick for several days. When I asked why no one had told me earlier, he informed me that he'd been calling leaving messages for me. I questioned Jonathan about it and he just shrugged his shoulders and said, "Your mom will be fine." Thankfully she recovered, because I never would've forgiven myself, or Jonathan, if something *more serious happened to her. That day, I got a cell phone and gave my number to my brother, my mom, and my best friend Sasha. I never told Jonathan about the phone; I got it under my name and paid for it with the allowance that he gave me every month.*

I was jolted out of my thoughts by a knock at my door. It was early, a little after 8 a.m., so I wondered who it could be. Through the glass pane window, I could make out the silhouettes of two men. Cracking the door just a little, I kept my foot positioned so the door couldn't open any further. The two men identified themselves as Detective Hodges and Detective Boatman of the Saint Louis Police Department; they were working on my husband's murder. Normally I would have asked for ID, but I recognized the older one from TV.

"Mrs. Skagel, may we come in?" Detective Hodges asked. "We have a couple questions concerning your husband's case."

My stomach tightening, I nodded and moved to the side so they could enter my home.

After offering them something to drink, which they politely declined, I gestured toward the living room sofa. They sat down, and I perched nervously on the edge of my recliner. The older one, Detective Hodges, sat directly in front of me and the younger one, Detective Boatman, sat on the far end of the sofa with his notepad in hand. Detective Hodges didn't waste any time getting to the point.

He leaned in and asked, "Mrs. Skagel, can you confirm your whereabouts on Friday, the night before your husband's murder?"

"I've already answered this question when the detective came to my house the day after my husband was found."

"Yes, but new evidence has been brought to our attention that we must address."

"What new evidence?" I questioned.

"Do you own a 2019 black Range Rover?"

"Yes…"

Detective Hodges laid a picture of a black Range Rover on the table. I knew exactly when and where this photo was taken, but there was no way I was going to admit this to them, especially since the picture was blurred.

"There are thousands of black SUVs, I can't be certain that that's my vehicle, where was this taken?" I questioned.

"It's from a convenience store right off the interstate, about an hour outside of Saint Louis," he stated, his eyes flicking over me. "It was taken the Friday night before your husband's murder."

I knew exactly what they were getting at and I wasn't about to budge.

He continued, "We also received a phone call putting you in the vicinity of Brookes Brothers on that night."

"Are you accusing me of something, detective?" I said coldly.

"I also spoke to your neighbor, Mrs. Sanders, who lives next door. She stated that she saw you leaving late afternoon Friday and that you returned Saturday after 2 p.m."

This was what they had, an unknown witness and Mrs. Sanders, an eighty-nine-year-old woman with dementia. She can't even remember what she had for dinner last night, but she can confirm my whereabouts from over a week ago? I chuckled inside because they were fishing and wasting my time.

"Mrs. Sanders has dementia; you can confirm that with her doctor."

Just then we heard a squeaky noise and looked towards the stairs to see Sophia. I didn't know how long she had been there but I didn't want her to hear anything more.

"You have to go now," I stated sternly.

"But we still have a couple more questions. Maybe we can step outside."

"No, I am done talking... You have to leave." I looked up at Sophia.

The detectives stood and started to walk towards the door, with me right behind them.

Detective Hodges turned to me. "Mrs. Skagel, this conversation isn't over."

"Yes, it is. You can schedule a meeting through my lawyer next time. Do not come to my house again." I closed the door, leaving them on my doorstep.

I turned to Sophia, who had made her way to the bottom of the staircase.

"Baby, are you okay?" I asked as I wrapped my arms around her.

"Did they find out who killed Daddy?" Sophia's voice was cracking.

"Not yet, baby."

"Then why were they here?"

"They just wanted to ask some questions; they won't be back."

I hugged Sophia, hoping that answer would satisfy her curiosity. She started to ask another question but thankfully was interrupted by Jonathan Jr. running down the stairs.

"Mom, can you make blueberry pancakes for breakfast?" he asked, wiping the sleep from his eyes.

"Sure, sweetie." I pulled him so I was hugging both kids at once. "I'm so glad to have my babies back at home. "I've missed y'all."

They hugged me back, "We missed you too, Mommy."

"Okay, you two go upstairs and wash your faces and I'll get started on those blueberry pancakes."

CHAPTER 16

VERONICA REDMOND

The meeting with Tanya went well, and she promised to be upfront with us from now on. Still, I had my work cut out for me. After the meeting, the Deacon and I discussed our plans for the next several days. He needed to go to the DA's office and I needed to start my investigation, we needed another vehicle, so Tanya agreed to lend me her car since she wasn't using it at this time. I decided to drive to the park where they found Jonathan's body. The entire section of the park was still blocked off. *Damn*, I thought, but on a hunch I quickly flashed my badge and was permitted by the young uniformed police officer, who apparently didn't notice that it was from another state, to pass through. Nice.

This was the secluded part of the park, which made me think Jonathan had been there to meet someone. I didn't want to get too close to the crime scene in fear of being identified and escorted off the premises, but since I was unfamiliar with Saint Louis, I wanted to get a general feel for the area. *Could this have been a random burglary? Or was this a case of Jonathan being at the wrong place at the wrong time?* The park was heavily wooded, and anyone not familiar with the area could easily get lost.

We knew that Jonathan was in town for a business meeting with some of the owners at Brookes Brothers, so I had spoken with Tanya about getting into the building. She told me that Mr. Charles Brookes had agreed to see me. David was to meet with the District Attorney about clearing Tanya's name due to the lack of evidence and to address how they arrested Tanya. David was right, the only thing they had was a watch which Jonathan could have gotten from Tanya's home the many times he was there. The case wasn't solid, and they knew it. They needed someone to blame until they found the real killer.

The next day, I made my way to Brookes Brothers. Aside from talking to Charles, I wanted to get a feel for how Tanya's coworkers felt about her and what they thought about the allegations.

I was greeted by a security guard as I entered the building. After I identified myself, he handed me a badge then gave brief directions to the office of Charles Brookes, which was located on the fifth floor. I stepped out of the elevator and was met by a bubbly redhead who introduced herself as Ginger, Tanya's assistant. She was overly eager to let me know how much she loved Tanya and how good of a boss Tanya was. I wasn't impressed by Ginger; in fact, I found her annoying. After a brief chat, she escorted me to the office of Charles Brookes. I had been expecting to meet the founder of the company and was surprised instead to see a handsome biracial man in his late thirties. It was Charles Brookes, Jr. the man from Tanya's Facebook photos. I shook his outstretched hand, then he led me to one of the chairs facing his desk before taking a seat behind it.

"Thank you so much for seeing me. Tanya speaks highly of you," I said.

He didn't say anything but nodded his head, a look of worry on his face.

"Are you alright? Is this still a good time?" I asked.

"I don't know, I just learned some disturbing news." He gave me a strange look.

At that moment, my phone vibrated; it was David. I pressed the ignore button because in my line of business when someone is ready to share something with you, you listen.

Charles continued. "I'm sure you're going to find this out anyway, so I might as well tell you what I know."

I scooted to the edge of my seat, giving Charles my undivided attention.

"I noticed several weeks ago that the accounts Jonathan personally handled weren't balancing, so I had Tanya look into it for me. Of course, I didn't know they had a relationship going on then."

My phone vibrated; it was David… again.

"Not now," I said silently and pressed the ignore button.

"It appeared," Charles continued, "that money was being moved from six accounts that Jonathan handled; the amount was a little over four hundred thousand. I've known Jonathan for over eight years, and even though I personally didn't trust him, my father thought highly of him. I knew there had to be an explanation, but when we questioned him the day before his death, he denied the whole thing. He appeared to be very upset about all of this."

"How can you miss over four hundred thousand from your accounts?" I asked.

"Exactly," Charles stated, "I wasn't going to be made a fool out of. My family worked too hard to build this company. I suspended him without pay on the spot, pending our internal investigation. Even if there was a mistake, his lack of focus isn't what this company needs. The look Jonathan gave me was of total despair, and he left my office without a word. I felt bad because I knew he had a family, but he left me no choice. Today, the temp accountant that I hired to cover for Tanya found that exact amount in a bank account that was closed over a year ago."

"What are you saying?" I asked.

"I'm saying that Tanya was the only one that had access to that account. She made Jonathan's accounts appear that he was sending money offshore, but she was actually moving it to this bank account. No one else had access to this account but her, and she was supposed to close it. Right before you came in I had a conversation with the head of our IT department, and he verified that the transfers came from Tanya's login information. The deposits started to hit the bank account a couple of weeks ago, and the dates match exactly to Jonathan's accounts. The amount that was in the account also matched the amounts missing from Jonathan's accounts. She set him up, but why?"

Charles looked like a wounded puppy, which reminded me of all the faces of guys from high school that Tanya used to get what she wanted. She always had a way of conning the good ones. I felt bad for Charles; he seemed to really care for Tanya. I sat in silence in disbelief of all this information.

"Did you say *was* in the account?" I questioned.

"Yes, apparently that money has been moved. My father is going to kill me!"

Charles lowered his gaze. "No one knows about this and I want to see if I can get to the bottom of it before it gets out."

"Do you think this is related to Jonathan's murder?"

"I don't know," Charles stated, his face red with embarrassment or fear, or something else altogether. I wondered what he was not telling me. Then he abruptly stood and extended his hand.

"I'm sorry, Veronica, but this is hitting me hard. Please call me if you have additional questions."

I stood as well and nodded. "I'll be in touch."

As I walked to the elevator pondering what I just learned, David called again.

"Sorry I didn't answer before but I have some new information that –"

David started to speak but by then I had stepped onto the elevator and the sound was garbled. I tapped my foot, impatiently waited the thirty seconds it took to make it to the lobby. Once the doors opened to the elevator, I quickly walked out, dropped the badge at the security guard and exited the double doors.

Once outside, I saw that the call was still active. "Hello David, I was in the elevator and had bad reception. Repeat what you said."

"I said, I'm leaving!"

"Leaving… to go somewhere for the case?"

"No, Veronica, I am done!"

I walked over to a nearby bench and sat down; he must have found out about Tanya moving money. That meant Charles must have lied, there was no way he just found out about Tanya's involvement with this.

"Imagine how I felt, walking into the DA's office to accuse them of an unlawful arrest, only to be blindsided by Tanya's scheming ways. Learning from the DA's office how she set Jonathan up by moving money from his account which caused his suspension. They have solid evidence that she did this. Never in my professional life have I been so humiliated. I have a reputation to uphold and after the conversation I had with Tanya the other day about her lying to me, she did it again!"

This was even worse than I thought.

"Veronica, I know Tanya is your friend," he began.

Former friend, I thought.

"But this case is going to blow up in our faces if things continue like this. She cannot be trusted. I suggest you think long and hard about your career if you choose to stay."

With that, he told me where to find the remaining files for the case and then he was gone.

I sat there in disbelief. How the hell had I gotten caught up in Tanya's scheme? I could be home relaxing enjoying my new city, but no… I am here, now alone, defending a woman whose innocence I was not yet convinced of. I needed to talk to Tanya, ASAP.

~ ~ ~

I decided to pay Tanya a visit. When I arrived, Mr. and Mrs. Jameson were there on the porch. They both stood up to greet me.

"Veronica dear," Mrs. Jameson said as she hugged me. "Please don't tell me that you're giving up on our Tanya too."

"Well she did lie," I said, "but no, I'm not giving up on this case just yet, though David had every right too."

Mrs. Jameson smirked at that comment, while Mr. Jameson nodded in agreement.

"It's difficult to defend someone when they are constantly lying to you," I added.

They both were silent. They would never admit that their precious daughter was a liar, let alone a killer.

I broke the awkward silence. "I came by to talk to Tanya."

"Sure dear, go right on in, she is up in her room," Mrs. Jameson said.

I walked upstairs to Tanya's bedroom and knocked. "Tanya, it's Veronica, I need to talk to you."

I didn't bother to bring up the money because Tanya knew David had already informed me. I really wanted to hear about her relationship with Jonathan. Tanya opened the door.

"Hi Veronica," Tanya stated. She looked like she had been crying. I decided to not fall for her tears; I needed the truth.

"Tanya, I need to talk to you about your relationship with Jonathan, I need details."

"Okay," she sniffed. "Come in."

I stepped into Tanya's bedroom, looked around and noticed how clean it was. Everything was in place. I walked over to the chaise that was by the window and took a seat.

"Tanya, again, I need to know everything about your relationship with Jonathan, from beginning to end. And tell me about the watch."

"That's the weird part," Tanya explained, "And I've been replaying it in my mind. I don't know how it got in the park. Every time I wore the watch, I always put it back in my jewelry box."

Tanya stood and walked to her dresser and grabbed the pink jewelry box and opened it. The ballerina twirled while music played.

"Do you remember this, Veronica?"

I smiled and said, "Yes, your dad gave it to you when you were seven."

"Yes, and I still love it." Tanya pulled out a necklace. "He gave this to me when I turned sixteen." Tanya put the necklace back in the jewelry box and placed it back on the dresser. "He gave me the watch when I graduated from graduate school," she turned to me, "Do you think they'll give it back to me once all of this is over?"

"Once the case is solved, they may, but I cannot say for sure," I stated.

Tanya frowned as she walked over to her bed and sat down. Instead of pressing for more information about Jonathan, I stayed and sat in silence with her for a few minutes, then decided to let her be.

An hour later, I was in my car headed back to the hotel. I had my work cut out for me. Mr. and Mrs. Jameson informed me as I was leaving that they were working on acquiring a new lawyer for Tanya and would let me know when they settled on one. I gave them my business card and asked that they give my information to the new attorney. The growling in my stomach erupted; this case had me going in all directions that I forgot to eat. The dinner at the hotel from the other night was great so I decided to order room service when I made it back.

While eating my meal, I reviewed the notes left by David. We had been trying to substantiate their relationship, prove it was more than just a hookup and an infatuation on Tanya's part. She and Jonathan first met at a conference in Charlotte, North Carolina. They immediately hit off at dinner that night. Since then, it seemed to be random meetups, until of course he proposed to her in the airport parking lot. From there they had gone to a cottage. Tanya had mentioned that

Jonathan wasn't feeling well when they arrived, so while he slept she went out for a walk around the lake. While she was walking, she met an elderly couple and they invited her to have drinks with them. But that information didn't do me any good, since the elderly couple never saw Jonathan.

I continued flipping through the papers and found nothing much to go on. I reread Tanya's statement and read about Samantha, the owner of the smoothie shop in the airport. Tanya mentioned that Samantha saw her and Jonathan in a shop at the airport. This was the only potential lead I had. As I continued flipping through the notes, my phone chirped. It was a text from David: *Just sent you an email of Tanya's phone records. You should look at it.*

I sent him a thank you, then opened my laptop, found his email, and clicked on the attachment. After several minutes of looking at the document, I picked up my phone and dialed David's number. He answered on the first ring.

"Veronica," he said my name in a relaxed tone.

"David, thanks for sending this to me and for answering my call."

"No problem."

"Is this the only phone line Tanya had, no work phone?"

"This is the only personal line. She has a different line for work and there were only a handful of calls on that line, none from Jonathan."

"It appears there weren't many calls from Jonathan on her personal line either."

"Exactly," David replied.

"This is interesting," I said, eyeing the Tequila on the bar.

"Things never added up with Tanya's story. Good luck with everything."

"Thank you, David," I said as I hung up the phone.

Over their three-month relationship, there were only two times Jonathan's number appeared on Tanya's phone bill. One was the day they met at the conference and the other one was the morning of Jonathan's death. I looked through the phone records and saw several text messages, but it was from unidentifiable numbers. Maybe Jonathan had another phone aside from his personal and work lines. Either Tanya was lying about her relationship with Jonathan or someone was going through a lot of trouble to make it appear that way. I needed answers. It was 6:15p.m., I hoped that smoothie shop was still open.

Thankfully the traffic was light and twenty minutes later, I was pulling into the parking lot of Saint Louis Lambert International Airport. I walked inside and quickly found the line of stores. As I kept walking, I saw the neon green S sign, with a smoothie cup twirling around. That must be it, I thought. As I got closer, I saw a tall, beautiful, athletic-type black woman standing behind the counter with a clipboard and a pen in her hand. She appeared to be taking some sort of inventory. I walked through the door and a buzzer chimed letting her know that someone entered her shop. She looked up from her notepad and smiled.

"Hello, may I help you?"

"Hi, are you Samantha, the owner?"

"That's me," she said, her smile broadening.

I reached out my hand and she grabbed it.

"Hi, I'm Veronica Redmond. I'm an associate of Tanya Jameson."

Samantha's body shifted.

I continued, "I'm sure that you have heard about her case on the news."

"Yes, I saw that. How can I help you?"

"She mentioned that the last time she was with Jonathan was here at the airport and that you may have seen them together, do you remember that?"

A beep chimed and we both looked towards the entrance of the shop to see a mother with a little boy. Samantha asked me if I could wait for a minute, then gestured for me to take a seat at the table next to the window. I could see why Tanya was comfortable with Samantha; she had an easiness about her. I watched as she interacted with the little boy, asking him what type of fruits he liked and making some suggestions to the woman. After making smoothies for both and completing their sale, Samantha walked to the table and sat in the chair across from me. She started fidgeting with her fingers.

What is she nervous about?

"What did you say your connection was to this case?"

"I'm a detective friend of Tanya's, just helping her out."

"I see," Samantha said and relaxed back in the chair. "That was the second time I saw Tanya; the first time was about four months prior when she was coming back from a business trip. She came in and purchased a smoothie. It was almost time for me to close, so I let her try several of the smoothies I had on hand. She was very nice; she was surprised that a black woman owned the shop. We talked about business and life, then she left. This last time was very weird."

"Weird, how so?" I asked.

"I spotted her in the scarf shop." She pointed to the scarf shop that was across the hall. "I noticed her because she seemed to be hiding from someone."

"Hiding? What do you mean?" I asked.

"I mean hiding, as in hiding behind a rack of scarfs and peering over the side." What prompted me to look that way was a light scream I heard from a woman's voice. When I looked up, I saw this man grab this woman from behind. They appeared to have known each other because she twirled around and kissed him. I didn't think anything of it, until I saw Tanya. She looked at me and gave me a weird smile. She appeared to be watching the couple, and as they moved she moved, continuing to hide. The man went to the counter and purchased the scarf the woman was looking at and then they left the store. Tanya followed them out the store."

"Can you describe how this man looked?" I asked.

"Very attractive black guy, tall, had on a nice business suit…"

"Do you mind if I show you a picture of someone?" I pulled out my phone and typed in the Brookes Brothers' website; I was glad they hadn't taken Jonathan's picture down because that was my only photo of him. "Is this him?" I turned my phone to show Samantha.

"Yes, that's the guy."

"And this woman, can you describe her?"

Samantha described a white woman, average height, with red hair.

"Red hair?" I said.

"Yes, and she looked young, maybe mid-twenties."

"Thank you, Samantha, you have been very helpful. I appreciate it."

"You are welcome," she said. "Do you think she did it?"

"That's what I'm trying to find out," I said as I stood up. I gave her my card in case she thought of anything else and then walked out of the shop. The only redhead I knew of was Ginger, Tanya's assistant, and she fit the description that Samantha just provided.

I was hoping that talking to Samantha would give me a clearer sense of Tanya's and Jonathan's relationship, but it had only made me more confused. I needed to speak with Ginger.

CHAPTER 17

VERONICA REDMOND

The next morning, I woke up early to go for a walk. I needed fresh air to wrap my mind around this case. I hadn't gotten much sleep last night. A lot of things didn't add up and if it didn't add up to me, it wouldn't add up to the District Attorney, which meant that Tanya could still be flying high on their radar. I hadn't heard back from Mr. and Mrs. Jameson on whether they'd hired a new attorney, but it had only been a day. As I exited the elevator of the hotel, the front desk clerk, Marie, waved me over.

"Detective, how's your stay going?" she asked.

She'd never addressed me that way before; how did she know I was a detective? In response to my curious look, she pointed to the T.V. that was hanging on the wall above the fireplace. A man was speaking, but I couldn't hear what he was saying because the volume was turned down low. Marie handed me the right side of her headphone; the other one stayed in her left ear. She must have sensed my hesitation because she whispered, "They're new," and held up the package with the hotel logo on them. I grabbed the dangling headphone out of her hand and put it in my ear.

"Like I stated, my client Tanya Jameson is innocent and I'm requesting the District Attorney to drop this interest in my client so she can move on with her life. The investigator on our team, Detective Veronica Redmond of the Atlanta Police Department, has solid evidence to eradicate any suspicion of my client". A picture of when I made Lead Detective flashed across the screen. I stood in total shock.

He continued "If this harassment of my client doesn't stop, we will be pressing charges against the Saint Louis Police Department and the District Attorney's office."

I took the plug out of my ear and handed it to Marie. "Thank you," I mumbled to her in disbelief.

"No problem," she stated as I began to walk away. "Also…." I stopped and turned to her. "Your hotel stay was extended for another week."

"Okay, thanks," I said and headed out of the hotel.

David was right; this case was getting messier by the day. I started my walk at a fast pace, trying to work through my anger. The nerve of this attorney for making a statement that included me, and the nerve of Mr. and Mrs. Jameson for not informing me that they had hired him! Like David, I too had a reputation to uphold and that reputation had now been placed in jeopardy. Plus that wasn't even a flattering pic of me. I needed to calm down before making any calls. My pace became faster and before long, I was running. I am not a runner, though, and it wasn't long before I stopped mid-stride gasping for air. Several people looked at me, probably wanting to call an ambulance. I leaned over, grabbing my stomach which was starting to cramp. A white older gentleman, in a neon yellow biking outfit, came over and handed me a bottle of water.

"Come take a seat," he said and guided me to a bench nearby.

"Thank you," I rasped, mortified but grateful for the help. I opened the room temperature water and took a gulp. He sat with me in silence until my breathing normalized.

"You will be okay, take it easy," he said and patted me on my hand, then stood and walked over to his bike.

Still too winded to talk, I waved to him as he rode off.

I slowly stood and began walking back to the hotel. The run had cleared my mind and I'd figured out how I was going to handle this situation. On my walk back, I called Brookes Brothers and pressed a series of numbers until I reached Ginger's extension. She answered in that annoying chipper voice, and after a brief conversation agreed to meet me for lunch.

~ ~ ~

Four hours later, I sat in a café a couple of blocks from Brookes Brothers, waiting on Ginger. I thought it would be best to meet outside the office. I wanted her to be totally honest with me about her relationship with Tanya…and possibly with Jonathan. After ten minutes

Ginger walked through the door of the restaurant. She glanced around and I waved my hand so she could see me.

"So sorry I am late, one of the VPs asked me for something as I was headed out," she stated as she approached.

"That's fine, I'm glad you agreed to meet with me to answer a couple of questions."

"Sure, anything to help Tanya." She flagged the waiter over.

We placed our orders, then I started by asking Ginger what type of boss Tanya was. Ginger raved on how Tanya always looked out for her and ensured that she got the raises she deserved, not stopping until the waiter brought our food.

"Sounds like she's a great boss," I said. "Did you notice any odd behaviors from Tanya?"

Ginger looked down at her turkey and cheese sandwich and gave a shoulder shrug.

I reached over and touched Ginger's hand. "It's okay, whatever you say will be between us."

"I heard Tanya's attorney on the T.V. earlier. He said that the charges will be dropped soon, so what's the point in bringing up stuff that doesn't matter?"

I cringed.

The attorney had made it seem like the case was all but closed and Tanya's innocence was proven. That wasn't true, but it was hard for me to override what he said. I am sure this was done intentionally; the Jamesons must have informed him of my doubts about Tanya's innocence and he wanted to cripple my investigation.

"Ginger, as the attorney said I am gathering information to prove Tanya's innocence, so anything you can tell me will help her."

Ginger visibly relaxed. "Well, there were some things that happened that didn't make sense."

"Like…" I prompted.

"Like Tanya ordering flowers for herself and having them delivered to the office, but most women do that so I didn't think anything of it."

"How did you find out that she was delivering them to herself?"

"Well, Tanya ordered from the same flower shop every time. I made friends with the delivery guy and he informed me that Tanya would place the orders herself."

"I see, what else?"

"Sometimes, I would hear her talking, but didn't see her phone light on or no one was in her office; it was like she was having an actual conversation with someone. When I would knock on her door, she would invite me in like nothing was wrong, so I would just let it be." Ginger paused. "She is really nice; I don't want to get her in trouble."

"You won't," I said. "I would like to ask you another question."

Ginger reluctantly nodded, and though I knew she was uncomfortable I needed to rip the band-aid off.

"How long were you and Jonathan in a romantic relationship?"

Ginger stared at me.

"How did you find out about that? It was Tanya wasn't it?"

"Wait, Tanya knew about your affair with Jonathan?" I asked, stunned.

She sighed, then leaned forward. "She found out on accident. We were trying to be discreet. About a month ago, one late evening, I thought everyone was gone but Tanya overheard my conversation with him. I confessed that I was dating a VP." Ginger looked at me, "Please don't tell anyone, detective, I could lose my job over this."

"Well if it'll help clear Tanya's name, there may be a possibility of this getting out, but I'll try my best to keep your name out of it."

Ginger put her hands to her face.

"How did Tanya react to you dating Jonathan?"

"What do you mean?"

"I mean, was she overly interested or concerned?"

"As a matter of fact, yes," Ginger said, perplexed. "She almost demanded a play-by-play description of all my interactions with him. I thought she was just being a big sister, was I wrong?"

Ginger began a trail of questioning that I didn't want her to go down, so I rerouted the conversation.

"So, tell me how you and Jonathan met."

"We met him a couple of years ago when I first started working at Brookes Brothers. He came here for a meeting with the VPs and we hit it off."

"Did you know he was married?"

"I didn't at first. I found out a couple of months later, but I didn't end it." She hung her head, clearly ashamed. "I knew he wasn't going to leave his wife – this wasn't my first time in a relationship with a married man. But Jonathan was fun and I enjoyed spending time with him. I didn't want that to end."

"Where would you go to meet up?"

"I would sometimes pick him up from the airport and we would go to a cottage about an hour away that my family owns."

"Did you see him the day of his murder?"

She hesitated.

"No. He called me, though, early that morning, saying that he knew who'd set him up and wanted me to ride with him somewhere. But I didn't think it was a good idea."

"Why not?"

"Lately I'd been feeling like someone was watching us. Jonathan thought I was paranoid, but I'd been in situations where the wife caught me with her husband, and it wasn't a pleasant experience. I wasn't taking any chances."

Ginger rubbed a healed scar on her forearm. I leaned back in my chair and when I looked at her again tears were coming down her face.

"If I was there, maybe he would still be alive."

"Or I could be trying to solve two murders," I said.

Ginger stared at me, then glanced at her watch. "I have to get back to the office, I hope you find out who did this to him," she said as she stood up.

"Oh, one other thing Ginger." I rose from my seat. "Can you tell me the phone number that Jonathan used to contact you?"

"It was always a different number; he used burner phones. He said it was best because of his wife. He would let the phone ring twice and then hang up. That's how I knew to call him back." She lowered her head and walked out the door.

I didn't have the guts to ask Ginger if he'd proposed to her. But she told me enough and confirmed what I thought. This was definitely a group of people that lies, but what were they covering up?

I was surprised that the District Attorney's office hadn't interviewed Ginger or made any mention of the phone records. Maybe Tanya's new attorney had a point; they didn't have enough to bring charges against Tanya officially or they would have done so by now.

When I got back to the hotel, Marie, the front desk clerk, informed me of a message from Mrs. Jameson on my room phone. I walked into my room and straight to the mini bar, where I poured a shot of tequila. I have drunk more in the last several days than I have in the last three months. After downing the shot I listened to the voicemail, in which I was informed that my services were no longer needed and that I could just leave Tanya's car at the hotel, they will pick it up later. Somehow, I had become a liability rather than an asset.

I sighed heavily and poured myself another shot, drank it, then I laid on the bed. David was right, these beds were amazing. I pulled out my phone and called Storm. He informed me that my paperwork was awaiting one signature and then my transfer would be complete. I knew this process would most likely take another two days. If I left now, I would have two days to enjoy the ocean before I get bogged down with the potential serial killer case.

With a sudden surge of energy, I stood up and started shoving clothes into my luggage. My work here was done. I knew that if I stayed any longer, and being the detective that I am, that I wouldn't stop until I discovered what happened that morning in the park. My job was to come and help Tanya, and I'd done that to the best of my ability. I'd also kept my promise to my mom, and I was okay with that. It was ultimately up to the District Attorney's office to convict the person who killed Jonathan. I just hoped Tanya wasn't that person.

I called Marie at the front desk and let her know that I would be checking out and needed a taxi to the airport. In this business, when it's time to let go, you just have to let go. David had reminded me of that.

On the way to the airport, something kept nudging at me. "Stop it," I told myself. "Go home, get some rest, they don't want you here."

The taxi stopped at a red light, right before entering the expressway. I turned my head to peer out the window and saw the lighted vacancy sign on The Sugarland Motel.

"Shit," I said out loud. The taxi driver glanced in the rearview mirror at me.

"Is everything okay ma'am? Did you forget something? I can turn around..." he stated in a thick accent.

"Unfortunately, it isn't okay. Can you let me out over there?" I pointed to the motel.

"You sure?"

"No, I am not sure," I said out loud while nodding my head yes.

When the light turned green, the taxi driver made a U-turn and pulled into the parking lot of the Sugarland hotel. I got out of the vehicle, and the taxi driver removed my luggage from the trunk and set it down. I thanked him, then handed him the fare and a generous tip. I couldn't believe what I was doing.

Once inside the motel I approached the front desk to get a room. I made my way down the long hallway to the last room on the right. It was a far cry from the Four Seasons; everything in the room was dingy and the bedspread definitely looked like it needed a good washing.

"Okay Veronica, prove Tanya's innocence and you can go home," I said out loud as I opened my luggage and pulled out the large folder I had on the case.

After several hours of reviewing the notes over and over again, my eyes were tired, my back ached and I was exhausted mentally and physically. I decided to walk to the diner next door to grab a quick bite to eat. I took a seat at the counter and an older blond woman approached me with a cup in one hand and a coffee pot in the other and poured me a cup of coffee. I nodded and brought the hot liquid to my lips. The waitress took my order and headed towards the kitchen.

I leaned back on the stool and took another sip of coffee, which was surprisingly good. There was something I was missing about this case. Suddenly, it came to me: I had been working it from the wrong angle all along. I'd been so busy working from the notes from David Mosley, which was geared towards proving Tanya's innocence, rather than solving a murder. My gut clenched with that familiar feeling I got every time I was onto something. I flagged down the waitress and told her to make my order to go.

With my food in hand, I entered my hotel room and clicked on the T.V. to see a photo of Tanya standing by her attorney on the screen. I stared in amazement as the newscaster announced that Tanya was officially no longer a person of interest in Jonathan's murder. The attorney's strategy had worked, and he was now in the process of suing the Saint Louis Police Department.

The detectives on this case weren't doing Jonathan justice. They hadn't even bothered to speak with Ginger and Charles, though they both had valuable information.

I thought back to the conversation with Ginger and realized something didn't sit quite right with me. I knew she was lying; her over-eagerness to impress me when I first visited the office and the way her eyes constantly shifted when we were in the café were clear signs of deceitfulness. Plus she had spent so much time gushing about Tanya, perhaps hoping that I would buy it as she tried to paint her as delusional. Then again, Charles had also pushed the attention towards Tanya, which was puzzling because it appeared that he truly had deep feelings for her.

After another day of running around Saint Louis, I uncovered more about this trilogy of Tanya, Charles, and Ginger than I had in the last several days. By talking to one of Charles' neighbors, I discovered that Charles' place was never being remodeled, which meant that he lied about why he needed to stay with Tanya. The more I thought about it, the creepier Charles appeared. His reaction to finding out that Tanya was the one who moved the money was that of total shock. My eagerness to get to the bottom of this was bringing out that fire inside of me and I needed to know what happened that day in the park.

I pulled up the Atlantic Police Database and prayed that my password was still active. When ACCESS DENIED appeared across my screen, I sighed, hoping this meant my transfer was close to being finalized. The alternative was that Morgan had found out about me accessing the database, which meant that Black was probably catching heat about this. To be sure it wasn't the latter, I picked up my cell phone and dialed Black's number.

"Two times in one week, to what do I owe this pleasure?" Black said, his voice unusually cheery.

An easiness came over me as I knew Black was most likely not in trouble for letting me access the database the other day. "Hi Black, how are things going?"

"The same, what's going on, partner?"

"I tried logging into the system and got an access denied message. I was worried."

"Oh yeah. I received notification this morning to disable your account; looks like the captain finally signed your transfer paperwork."

"Well that's good news, I was hoping we didn't get caught."

"Oh no, we are good on that."

"Excellent. Listen, I have a favor to ask."

Black laughed. "I figured as much. What do you need?"

"Does your pal from the academy still work at the Precinct in Saint Louis?"

"Yes, why?"

"Can you see if he will look up two names for me and see if any priors exist?"

"I haven't talked to him in a while, but I can try, let me get a pen." I heard rustling in the background, then Black came back to the line. "Okay, what are the names?"

"Ginger Spence and Charles Brookes Jr. Anything you can find will help me out. Thank you, I owe you."

"Yes, you do." Black laughed again. "I will get back to you shortly."

Later that night Storm called to inform me that my paperwork had come back a day sooner than expected and I was to report to work in two days. He also told me that the killer on Contigo Island had been arrested. I was thrilled that I wouldn't have to deal with that but frustrated that I would have to leave Saint Louis with the case unsolved. Hopefully Black would come through with some information that would help me make sense of it all. I had my expert opinion on what had happened in the park, but without hard evidence or authorization to be working the case, my hands were tied.

~ ~ ~

The next day, on my way to the airport, I decided to stop by the Saint Louis Police Department. To clear my conscience, I needed to share with the detectives what I discovered and my thoughts on the case. Jonathan was a cheater and a liar, but he was also a father and a husband and I wanted to give his family closure.

Black had called early this morning and I spent over an hour on the phone with him going over the case. Black informed me that both Ginger and Charles had records. Between the ages of sixteen and twenty Ginger had been arrested more than ten times for shoplifting but never convicted. I was sure this had everything to do with who her father was and his connections. They were minor charges, though, and I didn't see how they connected to the case.

Charles, on the other hand, had been in more serious trouble. Back in college he had stalked an ex-girlfriend, even violated several restraining orders. After breaking into her apartment he was arrested and wound up spending six months in county jail. His record had been clean since, but that might just mean he hadn't gotten caught; possessive behaviors rarely go away. This was big, considering how he doted on Tanya and had lied to her about his place being remodeled.

Unfortunately, I didn't have time to question Charles further and I doubted he would have talked to me again anyway. But I didn't need to talk to him; I had enough information to connect the dots. And I had that feeling in my gut again, letting me know that my hunch on what happened that day in the park was spot-on. Now I just hoped the detectives working the case would listen to me.

I walked into the precinct and asked to speak to Detective Hodges, the lead Detective on the case, saying I had information on a murder investigation. The officer asked me to have a seat in one of the orange plastic chairs along the wall. He then stood up and disappeared behind the glass doors. Fifteen minutes later, Detective Hodges appeared at the front desk.

"I can't talk to you," he stated.

"What do you mean? I have important information concerning the Skagel case." I stood up from my chair and walked over to him.

"Do you understand that we are now in a lawsuit because of Ms. Jameson? I cannot talk to you!" Detective Hodges turned to walk away.

"So that's it, you don't want to know?"

He turned back around to face me. "I've been doing this for over thirty years and I will get to the bottom of this, now if you don't mind, I have work to do. Have a good day, Detective Redmond!"

With that, Detective Hodges turned and walked down the long hallway. The desk officer, who had witnessed the entire exchange, looked up at me and shrugged. I asked for a marker and wrote in big letters "for DETECTIVE BOATMAN" on the manila envelope, then handed the envelope to the officer and asked him to give it to the detective. I hoped that he would investigate the information I had provided.

CHAPTER 18

VERONICA REDMOND

The flight back to Georgia was quiet and quick. I was excited that the case with Tanya was behind me. I could move forward with starting this new life of mine. I walked into my AIRBNB and let my luggage drop to the floor. I needed a long hot shower, but I was mentally and physically exhausted. I plopped in the chair and closed my eyes. The last week had seemed like two months. It was challenging and frustrating, but I learned a lot, about myself, and my former best friend.

My phone vibrated and I picked it up on the first ring without even looking at the caller ID.

"Hello?" I asked.

"Hi Detective," came the familiar thick accent. I sat up in my chair.

"Special Agent Christophe…"

"Please, call me Victor."

"Okay Victor, How can I help you?"

"I heard on the news that your friend was cleared, nice work."

I sighed knowing that he probably saw my photo on the news.

"Well, you're also due a pat on the back, it's nice that our small town is safe again, with that killer off the street. Storm was very pleased with your work."

The phone went silent and for a moment I thought it had dropped the call. It hadn't.

"Veronica, I was wondering if you would like to have dinner with me tonight. It's my last night before heading back to DC and thought you could use a nice meal."

I noticed the nervousness in his voice, and I was blushing.

"I would love to, but I just got in and don't think my legs could make it out the house."

"Well how about I bring dinner to you? I would love to cook you one of my favorite Jamaican meals."

"Ummm…"

"Don't worry, Storm can vouch for me; I am not crazy."

"At least not on paper you're not," I laughed. "I did my research!"

"Oh, I see!" he said, "So is that a yes? I can swing by the grocery store, pick up the items and be there by seven."

"Make it eight," I said, already thinking of my favorite Jamaican dish: curry shrimp, rice and peas and plantains. My stomach started to growl.

"Okay, see you soon."

~ ~ ~

Victor walked into my house, looking and smelling good and with a bagful of groceries in hand. I sat in my chair and enjoyed every minute of watching him prepare our meal. As we chatted I realized he was smart, funny, and possibly psychic, as he was making curried shrimp and plantains.

I was pleasantly pleased with the dish and his company. Victor was much different from "Special Agent Christophe." Victor was funny, sensual and a great cook, while Special Agent Christophe was firm, direct and smart. I liked both. After dinner, Victor asked if we could go outside. It was a beautiful night and the full moon lit the sky. We sat on my porch swing, enjoying the cool night breeze. This night couldn't have been more perfect, well almost. As Victor leaned in for a kiss, his phone rang. He blushed and pressed the green button, "Special Agent Christophe." I looked at him as his brow crumpled and he looked at me in astonishment. Several minutes later, he clicked the phone off and stared at me.

"Looks like I will be here much longer than expected, they found another body."

"What?" I exclaimed.

"Are you ready to join the team? I could use your help." He peered at me.

"I suppose," I said and Special Agent Christophe squinted. "I mean YES, Yes I am ready," this time with confidence.

Christophe replied, "Okay then let's go, I'll drive."

CHAPTER 19

Three months later

"Hi, Ma…" "Hey baby, I was so glad to hear you got that madman off the streets, how are you?" "I'm fine. The town is getting back to normal, How are you?"

"I'm okay, Veronica, I wanted to talk to you."

"Ma, please no more favors, you used all your favors up on Tanya."

"Oh hush, I'm not calling for any favors, but it is about Tanya. Her mom just called to let me that she got married."

"Married? "To who?" I asked.

"She bragged about her daughter marrying one of the owners of Brookes Brothers and how her daughter was doing so much better now."

I immediately thought of Charles and his disturbing background.

"Wow, well good for them, I hope it works out."

"That's all you have to say?" Mom asked.

"Yes Ma, that's all I have to say." There was a long pause, then my mom finally got to her real point.

"Oh, okay… well it's not too late for you to be in your sister's wedding."

"Ma, please…"

"Okay, okay, V … I'm just glad you are coming. You *are* still coming, right?"

"Yes, I will be there."

"Will you be bringing your new friend?"

"Maybe…"

"Oh great! See you this weekend, sweetie."

CHAPTER 20

CHARLES BROOKES JR.

Tanya and I had been married for two weeks and I couldn't be happier. I knew about the money she'd moved from the accounts, but I didn't tell her that. I didn't want to rock the boat. Besides, Tanya was really hurt by Jonathan and his lies, so I understood why she did what she did.

After she was cleared of all suspicions, we started to get closer. She was no longer working at Brookes Brothers so I decided to come clean about my feelings for her. She admitted she'd felt the same way. After two and a half months of dating, we eloped. My dad wasn't too happy about it and my friends thought I was a fool. But I'd loved Tanya from the moment she walked into my office for her interview fifteen years ago. Call it love at first sight, I knew she would be my wife one day.

I could hear the water running in the shower. Tanya and I just spent a beautiful night together. Today we leave for our honeymoon to the Maldives. My phone rang. As I reached to grab it, I knocked my phone off the nightstand along with Tanya's journal. Tanya wrote in this journal every day. I forgot about the phone ringing and was transfixed on the journal laying open on the floor. It was opened to the page dated June 26th – the date of Jonathan's death. I knew it was wrong to read someone's personal journal, but the way it had fallen open to that page, well it couldn't be a coincidence. The shower was still running so I picked the journal up and read it:

June 26th

My intentions weren't to kill Jonathan. I just wanted to talk to him. I was hurting and needed answers. I didn't want to talk to him over the phone, this conversation needed to happen in person. Why did he do what he did to me? Did he even love me? Was our relationship a joke? These are all the questions I needed answers to. Jonathan didn't even tell me he was coming in town for a meeting, I learned that from Ginger. It had been two weeks since

I found out about Jonathan's other life and in that two weeks, I moved $438,000 from his account to an old company's savings account. That account was supposed to have closed months ago, but I honestly forgot to close it. It completely slipped my mind, until I received an email from the bank. I knew what I wanted to do but didn't know how to fully execute my plan until I received the email. It was perfect. I figured that I would start with $25,000 to get Jonathan's attention. Then $50,000. Surely, he would notice the money missing and ask for help. Then I would go to Chicago to help him figure it out and get the answers I needed. But before I knew it, I had moved $438,000 and he never figured it out. I guess he wasn't the efficient businessman I thought he was. I just wanted to get his attention; I never intended for things to get out of hand like they did.

Charles, being the brilliant man that he is, noticed the discrepancy on Jonathan's last report and started his own investigation. Jonathan had been accused of forging and reporting inaccurate numbers. When Charles asked about it, I lied. Of course, I said I would look into it. My plan was to put the money back and let Charles know that it was a banking error. But everything happened so fast. A real emergency at the office in Charlotte had occurred, so I had to fly there and when I came back,

Charles had started his own investigation. It would've been too risky for me to do anything at that point.

Since finding out that Jonathan was married, he attempted to call me a couple of times, and I briefly spoke to him once, but I needed to see him, to look him in his eyes. I knew I was too weak to hear his excuses over the phone; I would have easily fallen for his lies. The Friday when Jonathan was to arrive at the office for his 9a.m. meeting, I made sure to be in Charles' office around that time. At 8:45a.m., I walked into Charles' office to ask a question about the Charlotte office. Charles wasn't his usual happy-go-lucky self; I could tell that the upcoming meeting with Jonathan was bothering him. After a couple of minutes of random questions, Charles stated that he had a meeting and that he would call me as soon as it was over. I looked at the clock it was 8:50am, I was hoping to stay in Charles' office until Jonathan showed up; I guess I would just have to see him another way. As I opened the door to leave, I smelt the scent of Jonathan. I looked up and there he was, standing there, talking to – or shall I say flirting with – Charles' assistant, Renee. Jonathan looked at me with a smirky grin on his face, his arrogance was disgusting. I couldn't believe I didn't see this before. Charles came up behind me, "Jonathan, good, you're here, you know Tanya, right?" "Yes, we've met," Jonathan, said as he reached out to shake my hand. I looked at him and shook his hand. "Nice to see you again," he said then turned to Charles, "Are you ready or should I wait?" "Actually, we'll be meeting in the conference room, let me grab my iPad and I'll walk with you, the others should be there shortly." I walked back to my office, hoping that he got whatever came to him.

I went home that evening frustrated at how I allowed myself to get caught up like this. I stared at the ring Jonathan proposed to me with a couple of weeks ago. I should've just pawned it and booked myself a much-needed vacation. But I didn't think of that, I was fuming and needed closure.

The next day, I got up early to go for my usual Saturday morning jog. Mid-jog, my phone rang, I slowed my pace and answered it.

It was Jonathan, asking if we could meet up, he wanted to discuss something. This was the call I'd been waiting for; it was time. I told him to meet me at Forest Hill Park, Pavilion 49, at 9 a.m. I knew that park well and knew it would be isolated around that time. I wanted privacy with Jonathan so he could tell me the truth. I finished my jog, hopped in the shower and headed out to meet Jonathan.

Jonathan was parked right in front of Pavilion 49 when I rolled up around 9:15. I don't know what made me ride my bike to the park instead of driving. I don't know why I wore a black hoody or why I brought a gun. I still ask myself this to this day. I stopped my bike and laid it against the tree. Jonathan got out of his car and walked to me. He hugged me and whispered hello in my ear. I embraced him back, he felt different but it was nice being in his arms. It started to sprinkle; I didn't consider the rain when I rode my bike here. Jonathan asked if we could sit in his car to talk, I nodded and walked to the passenger side of the car and got in. Once in the car, there was silence. I looked out the window as the beads of rain started to roll down.

I asked Jonathan what he wanted to see me about. He immediately went in trying to play down our relationship, making me think that I made the whole thing up. I became livid and confronted him about his wife, "Jonathan just stop, I know about your wife and kids. What I don't know… is why? Why lead me on like this?"

He continued denying our relationship. I held up my hand so he could view the ring that I still wore on my finger. "You are a joke! I thought we had something special and you obviously did too, or you wouldn't have proposed to me!" I saw the look on Jonathan's face, it was a glimpse of the man that laid in the bed next to me *looking in my eyes, masculine but vulnerable. This was the Jonathan I had fallen in love with.*

I stared forward, looking at the raindrops that now matched the tears that were streaming down my face. The clicking noise of doors locking alerted me. I glanced at Jonathan in fear. He glared at me with piercing eyes.

He was angry, very angry. I'd never seen this side of Jonathan before and I had to admit I was afraid of him. He stated that he didn't have time to play these games with me and told me he knew I was behind the money transfers.

I denied it at first but then came clean. "Screw you, Jonathan! Yes, I set you up! And you deserved it! I hope you get everything that's coming to you!" I pulled the handle on the door.

The door swung open and drops of rain began to cover my right arm. I put my hand in my jacket pocket and started to leave when Jonathan forcefully grabbed my left arm. He wanted me to tell Charles everything, he wanted me to clear his name, but there was no way I was going down with him. I tried yanking my arm away, but his grip was so strong that yanking my arm only made me scream in pain.

I finally freed my arm from Jonathan's grip. Jonathan lunged at me. I felt the cold steel of the gun in my pocket. Without thinking, I pulled the gun out and shot him. The bullet hit him right in the chest. Jonathan stared at me as he slowly fell back against the door. He grabbed his chest and look at his hand as it was covered in blood. I shoved the gun in my jacket pocket and quickly got out of the car, not knowing if Jonathan was dead or alive. The rain started to come down heavy. I hopped on my bike and rode through the wooded trail. The rain became a thunderstorm, so I peddled faster; I needed to get out of this park.

As I got about two blocks from my home, I was soaked. I took my bike and laid it on a side of some random house where there were a couple of other bikes. I walked the rest of the way home. Once inside, I felt my pockets for the gun, but it wasn't there, it must have fallen out. I thought about retracing my steps to locate the gun, but that would've been too risky. I walked to my bedroom, sat on the floor and screamed. I felt like I had been holding my breath since the park. I couldn't believe it... I had just killed Jonathan.

The sound of the water shutting off jolted me back to reality. I quickly closed the journal and placed it back on the nightstand. I stood up and started pacing; I was at a loss for words. I wanted to tell Tanya that I knew the truth, but I didn't know how she would take it, and I couldn't lose her. Tanya came out of the bathroom naked and soaking wet. I stared at her, watching her every move. She walked over to the freshly folded towels and grabbed one.

She started drying off her body and looked up at me, "What's wrong, babe? You look like you just got bad news."

I couldn't speak, I just looked at her in silence.

Tanya walked over and stood next to me. She started rubbing my back, "Babe, you okay?" she said in my ear and planted a soft kiss on my neck.

I quickly turned with the touch of Tanya's lips on me. "I'm fine, just an annoying business call."

"Oh, do you want to talk about it?"

"No, not now."

Tanya finished drying off and walked over to the dresser and pulled out a pair of thongs and slid them on.

"Well, we have to start packing now or we are going to miss our flight."

I nodded and walked to the closet to retrieve our suitcases.

CHAPTER 21

GINGER SPENCE

I walked into the large office, still unable to believe it was really mine. Brookes Brothers had made a lot of changes in the last several months. They restructured most of the departments and added more midlevel management to handle various accounts, instead of the directors being over all the accounts in their branch. I was now the Executive Assistant to the VP of Marketing. There was also a policy prohibiting workplace relationships between executives and those who worked for them. After all the drama that had gone on around here I was sure that wouldn't be a problem anytime soon.

Rumors were still circulating through the office about Charles and Tanya's marriage. Most people believed that Tanya killed Jonathan, especially since the four hundred and thirty-eight thousand had never been recovered. Everyone knew that Charles was madly in love with Tanya; I guess Tanya felt the same way about him.

Jonathan's multiple affairs throughout Brookes Brothers were discovered, hence the reason for the new policy. Apparently, he was having another affair with a young assistant in his office, which didn't surprise me. They didn't have enough evidence to bring charges against Tanya, so the interest in her were dropped. Her lawyer was able to even get the District Attorney's office to submit a formal apology. Shortly after Tanya was cleared, she turned in her notice at Brookes Brothers, then the rumors started about Charles and Tanya dating. Rumors that obviously turned out to be true.

For two weeks after talking to Detective Veronica Redmond, I was on pins and needles. I jumped every time the phone or doorbell rang, afraid the cops had found out about my lies, especially the lies I'd told about Tanya. Sure, she'd been ordering flowers for herself, but she wasn't crazy. She just liked flowers. Now that I thought about it, she never once made it seem like the flowers were from someone; she would just take them, smell them, and put them in a vase. After I found out about Jonathan's multiple affairs, I regretted helping him try to make Tanya look paranoid and crazy in love with him.

I waited for the detectives to come knocking on my door or worse, show up at the office, but they never did. My name was never mentioned as a person that Jonathan was having an affair with. Detective Redmond had been true to her word about that.

When she called and asked me to meet her for lunch I knew she had talked to Samantha. Samantha and I were close friends from college, and she was the only person I told about Jonathan. She called me when she saw Tanya and Jonathan at the airport that day, and that's when I learned of their affair. Jonathan had just been with me; in fact, I was the one who dropped him off at the airport. I envied their relationship because I knew it was much deeper than the one I had with him would ever be, so when I got a chance to try to break them up I took it. I found out that Tanya was setting Jonathan up and told him about it.

I didn't realize it at first, but when Tanya started staying late at work and being jumpy I figured she was up to something. I forgot my phone in the office one evening and drove back to get it. When I walked in, I noticed that Tanya's office lights were still on, so I knocked on her door. No response. I walked in and saw her computer was still on; she must have just left. I glanced around the office, looking for nothing in particular; I was just curious about what she'd been working on these late evenings. I didn't see anything out of the ordinary so I started to leave; that's when a blinking light coming from the laptop caught my eye. I walked over and clicked on the blinking notification. A transfer pending status popped up on the screen. This was weird because it was to a bank account under Brookes Brothers' name but one I didn't recognize. Grabbing a piece of paper and a pen, I wrote down the bank information then quickly left her office.

For the next several days, I started paying attention to the email notifications that came from that bank. At first I thought Tanya was stealing the money for herself so I just kept quiet and watched the money being deposited. Then the rumors started amongst the secretaries about the missing monies from Jonathan's account. That's when I started keeping records. Jonathan was sneaky but he was no thief, and he loved his job at Brookes Brothers. After seeing the latest statement from the bank and comparing it to the amount Ruby from Jonathan's office had stated was missing, I put two and two together. I was furious at Tanya for setting him up. How could she do that to him? He was married with kids; he could lose everything. I called Jonathan that day and told him that I had important information he should know. That's when we came up with the plan to prove that Tanya was delusional.

I remembered that Samantha stated she saw them at the airport. I offered her money to lie about seeing me with Jonathan that day, which she jumped at because her smoothie shop was in debt by thirty thousand. She felt bad because she thought Tanya was a really nice person, but once I assured her that no one was going to get hurt – and reminded her of the possibility of losing her precious smoothie shop – she agreed. Of course, at this time we never thought that anyone would die. We just wanted to prove that Tanya was obsessed with Jonathan and would go to any lengths to destroy him.

At the café that day Detective Redmond was getting too close. When I realized she knew about my affair with Jonathan it was time for me to leave. Of course I had known it was only a matter of time before someone figured it all out, but I thought for sure it would be the detectives working the case. Turned out they weren't interested at all in Jonathan's affairs. They were just into learning everything about Tanya. The older detective contacted me a couple of times, but he just wanted to talk about Tanya; he never asked anything about me. The younger one was new and didn't know what to ask. I figured this was his first case as a detective. I told them the same thing I'd told Detective Redmond, that Tanya was a nice boss.

Everything I said to Detective Redmond was true, all except for agreeing to meet Jonathan the morning of his murder. I knew he was going to meet Tanya, because that was the plan. Jonathan and I knew she would agree to meet up with him. She fell hard for Jonathan's smooth-talking. Jonathan knew I saw through his bullshit and didn't try to run game. Our relationship was about sex and having fun. I didn't care to hear about his problems, and he knew this. I guess Tanya was different. I wondered if he loved her.

Three days before Jonathan came to town, I found out I was pregnant. This was the day after I met up with him to tell him about Tanya. Although I was dating other men, I knew Jonathan was the father, the timing added up. The last time I was with him was a month ago and I haven't been with anyone else since then. At first, I wasn't going to tell him because I didn't even know if I wanted to keep the baby. Me having a baby by a married man? I could only imagine the rumors in the office, and my father would disown me for ruining the family's name.

Jonathan texted me the moment after he was put on suspension. The text read, "GAME ON." I'd been calling him for the last two days. I wanted to inform him that I was pregnant and couldn't go through with setting Tanya up. I wanted out of this charade with him. On the day of his murder, Jonathan called me wanting me to confirm our plans and to tell me the location.

"So, all you care about is your job?"

"Look Ginger, I have been under a lot of pressure lately… can't you see this?"

"I can see that you are selfish; plus, you had the audacity to ignore my calls and messages. Now you want me to be a witness to you being set up?"

"Yes, we are meeting at Forest Hill Park, Pavilion 49, at nine a.m."

"Wow, it's all about you! I don't know how you will ever be a great father to our child!"

"What!?"

"Yes, I am pregnant. You would know this if you returned my calls."

"Ginger, I don't have time for this bullshit. How do I even know the baby is mine? You have multiple men… yes, I know about them."

"Whatever, Jonathan!" I'd said and hung up the phone.

I was beyond frustrated. How could he just blow me off like that? I decided at that moment that I would go to the park, not as a witness for Jonathan but to confront him. I didn't give a damn about his job; I just wanted to know if he was going to be a father to our child.

~That day in the park~

The rain started to come down hard as I entered the park. It was around 9:25 a.m. and I wondered if Jonathan was still here. I wasn't familiar with this park, so I had no idea where I was going. The heavy rain was making it hard to see the signs. After driving around randomly for ten minutes, I saw a car parked in front of a pavilion. I figured that had to be Jonathan. I didn't see another car, so I assumed that Tanya hadn't arrived yet. I parked my car at the pavilion across from where Jonathan was, grabbed my green raincoat, and started walking to his car. I wanted to catch him off guard. As I walked closer to the car, I was startled by the sound of a gunshot. I stopped in my tracks and looked in the direction of Jonathan's vehicle. The rain was coming down harder, but I was able to make out a shadowy figure in a hoody exiting the passenger side. They ran over to a bike that was laying against a tree. I hadn't even noticed that bike before. Was that Tanya? The height and size were right, but I couldn't see clearly with the heavy rain. The shadowy figure got on the bike and disappeared into the woods.

Looking around to make sure the person wasn't coming back, I slowly walked to the opened passenger side door of the vehicle. Inside, Jonathan was slumped against the driver's side door, holding his chest and gasping for air. He looked at me like I was his savior; I think I actually saw a smile come across his face. He pointed a bloody finger at the cell phone in my hand. He wanted me to call for help. I glanced from my phone to him and back again, then keyed 911. Jonathan looked at me with relief; he didn't know that instead of hitting the green call button, I had hit the home button. If I called for help I would have to explain why I was there and the affair I had been having with Jonathan. And then what? My father, owner of the biggest construction company in Saint Louis, would disown me and my life would be over. Not like I could trust Jonathan; he'd eventually turn on me just like he turned on everyone else. I looked at him, then closed the passenger door and walked to my own car. It was only a short drive to the clinic.

CHAPTER 22

SYLVIA S. SKAGEL

The detectives' assumptions were correct. They came to my house questioning my whereabouts the day before Jonathan's murder. That was my SUV in that picture. I didn't believe Jonathan when he stated that he had an important meeting with the senior team in Saint Louis. He'd been traveling to Saint Louis more than usual over the past three months. So when he phoned earlier that morning stating that he was headed to Saint Louis for another meeting, I was pissed. First, because he failed to mention it the night before because he knew I would have a problem with it and, secondly because he'd just gotten back from Saint Louis the week before. The kids were on their break and we were all supposed to head to Six Flags that day. He did this on purpose; he didn't even have the decency to let the kids know he wouldn't be able to make it.

Luckily, that morning Sophia came into my room and mentioned that her best friend Kayla's family was going to Six Flags and asked if she and her brother could go with them. She was hesitant to ask because she knew we were going as a family. I pretended to be upset but said it was okay. I then called Kayla's mom, who explained it was for Kayla's birthday and that they were having a sleepover that night as well. *Wow, this is working out perfectly*, I thought. Kayla, her parents and her little brother arrived at my house around noon to pick up the kids. I handed Sophia money, kissed my kids on their foreheads, and gave a friendly wave to the parents as they backed out of my driveway; then I put my plan into action. The goal wasn't to confront Jonathan but to gather evidence for a divorce. If I could produce physical evidence of his affair I would have an easier time getting everything I deserved.

A couple of weeks earlier when I visited my divorce attorney, she'd asked me if I had any evidence of Jonathan's recent affairs. I said no, and she informed me that it would be hard to prove his infidelity in court without it. She gave me the numbers of a couple of P.I.s

I could hire to follow Jonathan, but after finding out their prices I figured I would try to get the evidence myself. One P.I. had advised me to put a tracker on his car. I thought about that but decided to put it on his laptop instead because he never went anywhere without it. The tracker was nice and sleek and, thanks to a couple of YouTube videos I was able to install it in the battery compartment.

I went upstairs to Sophia's bedroom and took the camera her dad had bought for her last year off the bookshelf. The camera was such an expensive gift for a nine-year-old, who, on a whim, had decided that she wanted to be a photographer. Jonathan believed in buying the best for our kids. That hobby lasted for one month and since then that camera had sat on her bookshelf collecting dust. I turned it on, surprised when it immediately came to life. I guess buying the best really did pay off. I took a couple of photos around the house and used the zoom feature to make sure I could be at a safe distance when capturing Jonathan's scandalous ways. I hurriedly dressed in all black because that's what I'd seen in the movies, then gathered my belongings, the binoculars, camera, and hoody sweatshirt. I was out of the house by two, plenty of time to beat the rush hour traffic. Over the four-hour drive I didn't listen to any music; I just focused on what I would do when I saw him with her, whoever she was. I mentally patted myself on the back for placing the tracker in his laptop, because for some odd reason Jonathan had decided to rent a vehicle for this trip instead of driving his own.

As I approached the outskirts of Saint Louis I pulled over at a convenience store to check Jonathan's location. According to the app he wasn't that far from me, only forty minutes. I got back on the road and a little over a half-hour later had reached the parking garage of Brookes Brothers. That's when my phone vibrated. It was him! I looked around, wondering if he had spotted me.

"Hello?" I answered hesitantly.

"Hey, babe…"

I pulled into the garage and saw Jonathan, standing outside of his car looking defeated. I guessed he really had gone to that meeting. Jonathan spoke to me for about ten minutes, for the first time opening up about his job, including his recent suspension. He sounded like he was truly heartbroken. It took everything out of me not to park my car, run to him and wrap my arms around him. Then I noticed someone, a man, walking to his car. Jonathan told me I shouldn't worry, that he would get to the bottom of things, then he ended the call. I placed the phone on the passenger seat and watched as Jonathan turned toward the man. As they stood there talking, I pulled out the camera and clicked the zoom button for a closer view. The man handed him something, which appeared to be a USB. Jonathan reached into his car and pulled out his laptop, then stuck the USB into the port. Whatever was on there wasn't good news. Jonathan slammed the laptop closed and tossed it onto the back seat, then got behind the wheel and sped off. I decided to let him leave and not follow too closely; the last thing I need was for him to spot me.

Fifteen minutes later, I pulled into the parking lot across the street from the Sugarland Motel and watched Jonathan walk into the lobby. A moment later he came back out with a key in his hand. He grabbed his laptop and overnight bag from the backseat, then proceeded up the stairs to Room 224. *This is classy*, I thought sarcastically. I wondered what trash of a woman would meet at this place. I made a mental note to get myself an STD test when I got back to Chicago.

Jonathan entered his motel room, then switched on the lights. I watched and waited but saw nothing, no sign of anyone. After forty-five minutes, I decided to walk to the diner I had seen on the corner to order food and use the restroom. I wasn't sure what I was going to do when I saw the woman he'd been having an affair with; hopefully I'd have the control to get my evidence and head home. I got the food and went back into my SUV. The night was quiet; the only action was that of a guy delivering a pizza to Jonathan's room. I grunted in frustration. Of all the nights I could have followed him, I had to choose the one when he was telling the truth!

After three hours of watching, the lights in Jonathan's room went dark. A second later my phone buzzed with a text from him: "Babe, it's been a busy day. I will be home tomorrow. I love you." I texted back, "Love you." And it was true. Even after all he had put me through, I still loved him. Suddenly, all the anger drained out of me, leaving nothing but exhaustion. I decided that I would take a short nap in the car before heading back to the house.

The voice of a man and woman having a very loud argument woke me up. I opened my eyes and saw the inebriated couple standing outside of the room directly under Jonathan's floor. I glanced at the clock; it was 6:37 a.m. The day was overcast, with huge dark clouds that promised rain. Oh my gosh, I couldn't believe I slept that long. Dotting my eyes across the parking lot frantically until I spotted Jonathan's rental car still in the same spot, I exhaled. He was still there. If he made it home before I did I'd have a lot of explaining to do. I started my car and was about to drive off when I noticed through the thin dingy curtains that the light in Jonathan's room was now on. I turned the car off again and grabbed the camera to zoom in but there was nothing to see.

The area started to get more movement; several people were coming out of the motel and walking over to the diner. Others were loading their car up, heading home or to their next destination. For a moment I sat there, torn about what to do. Part of me was saying I should admit my "mission" had been a failure and head home, but the other, bigger part won out. I had to know what Jonathan was up to, why he was still here. With a sigh, I decided to give it a while longer. A while turned into a couple of hours, and still there was no movement from Jonathan's room. I yawned and rubbed my lower back, which had begun to ache. *This is hard work*, I thought, *maybe I should've just hired a P.I.* I looked at myself in the rearview mirror, noting my disheveled hair and the bags under my eyes, then grabbed my baseball cap from the back seat and put it on my head. I would need coffee for the drive back to Chicago, and that meant another walk to the diner. I stretched my arms over my head, then glanced at my reflection again and groaned. Thank God no one around here knew me.

Ten minutes later, I exited the diner, hot coffee hand; a few sips and I was already starting to perk up. Suddenly, I saw Jonathan's rental pass by and ducked behind a truck that was pulling up, fully expecting him to turn around and ask what the hell I was doing there. He didn't, but I got pretty strange looks from the man and woman getting out of the truck. I smiled and pulled the hat down further over my head, then quickly made my way to my vehicle and jumped in. I pulled out my phone and opened the app, waiting for a beat as it located Jonathan, then started the car and pulled out of the lot.

It took a minute for me to catch up with Jonathan; he was speeding as if in a rush to get somewhere and from the direction he was headed it was definitely not home. I followed a few cars behind him and was surprised when ten minutes later he pulled into a wooded park. Sure he was going to see me, I slowed up so there was more distance between us. Unfortunately I slowed up too much because when I entered the park I no longer saw his car. *Damn.* I kept driving until I came to a four-way stop, then glanced at my phone and saw the signal fading in and out.

"Dammit!" I said out loud.

For about ten minutes I sat there at the stop sign, waving my phone around trying to pick up a signal, but no luck. I definitely didn't want to get lost in here; it was a creepy park, with big trees and very desolate.

Out of nowhere, I saw a person on a bike riding through the wooded trails. It was probably just someone out for their morning ride, but something about it struck me as odd, maybe because of the lousy weather. The bike was a regular ten-speed, and they were having a hard time pedaling over the rough terrain.

I pulled over and parked on the side of the road, then grabbed my camera and my sweatshirt. Just then it started to rain in fat chilly drops. *I must be crazy,* I thought as I started following on foot, yet something kept telling me it wasn't a coincidence that this person was here the same time as Jonathan. I studied the figure and despite the nondescript clothes decided it could definitely be a woman. Whoever it was continued to struggle, making it easy for me to keep up. Finally, they came to a stop and that's when I noticed Jonathan's rental car. I was finally going to get the evidence I needed. I hid behind a tree and pulled the cover off the camera, ready to catch my husband in the act.

Jonathan got out of the vehicle and walked over to the person on the bike, greeting them with a tight embrace. I snapped a photo. This had to be the woman he'd been having an affair with. She walked to the passenger side of the car and got in while Jonathan slipped back behind the wheel. The rain started coming down harder. I stooped under the tree to shield myself from the heavy rainfall and pulled my hat further down my head. I heard a door open, but no one got out. A few minutes later another car drove up and the person, clearly a woman, turned the headlights off. Snap. This was becoming weirder.

What the hell is going on?

I peered at her through the camera and saw that she was staring at Jonathan's car. Snap- Snap. She then got out of her vehicle, slipped into a lime-green raincoat she'd pulled from the back seat and started walking toward Jonathan. Snap. *Who is this woman, and why was she here? Was this a love triangle?* I wouldn't put it past my husband to be carrying on with more than one person; he'd done it before.

I was startled by a pop-pop coming from Jonathan's vehicle. It sounded like a gunshot. My heart pounding, I watched as the person who'd been riding the bike quickly exited the passenger side. They tightened the hoody, but I got a flash of the face; yes, it was definitely a woman. Keeping her head down, she walked over to the bike and peddled off. Snap – Snap – Snap.

Had she just shot Jonathan?

Without thinking, I stood and started to move in the direction of his car, but stopped when I saw the woman in the green raincoat also headed that way. I leaned back against the tree, watching as she approached the open passenger-side door. She stared into the vehicle for several minutes. I zoomed the camera in on her. *What is she doing? Why isn't she calling the cops? Why wasn't I calling the cops?"* Snap-Snap.

The woman closed the passenger door. Snap. She looked my way, and I thought she'd heard the click of the camera, but no; her face was glazed over, strains of her red hair stuck to her face. Snap-Snap-Snap. She walked to her car, got in, and drove away.

I stood there for a moment, shocked, soaked and shaking. Based on the woman's demeanor, I knew Jonathan was dead. Once she drove away, I walked from under the tree to my SUV, got in, and began driving out of the park. I didn't have an answer as to why I didn't call the police. I was so confused at this point. I drove around randomly for an hour, shivering and wishing I had more coffee. *I've got to get out of these wet clothes* I thought. I spotted a local Walmart and went in, purchasing a towel and a light pant set. I went into the restroom, changed my clothes, put my wet ones in the trash and walked out of the store. The tears started a half-hour into my drive and I was still crying when I pulled into my driveway five hours later.

Around four o'clock I received the call from the Saint Louis Police Department; they'd found a man's body with my husband's identification in a local park. The policewoman asked me how soon I could be there to identify the body. I called my parents, breaking down several times as I gave them the news. They offered to take me to Saint Louis, but I wanted them to be here when the kids arrived home from their sleepover. I then called my girlfriend from the gym and asked her to come with me to identify the body. Thankfully she said yes because I don't know how I would have done it alone. Even with her there, I almost passed out of the sight of him; worse, I knew I would have to live with that image for the rest of my life. By the time we got back to my house it was early morning. My parents had left a note saying they were taking the kids with them. I was relieved at that, not knowing if I could face them.

~ ~ ~

Several days later my shock and sadness turned to anger when I found out that Jonathan's insurance policy had lapsed. Not only had this person taken my husband from me and the kids, she had caused us to be in financial strains as well. The more I worked on the spreadsheet Kevin provided for me, the angrier I became, but now the anger was directed at my husband. Based on my calculations, it would take half my savings to bring us current on the bills. How could he let the policy lapse?

Needing a distraction, I turned on the T.V. and started flipping through the channels, looking for the Food Network. Watching other people cook always relaxed me. As I passed a news channel, the words on the bottom of the screen stopped me in my tracks. *Person of interest arrested in Saint Louis murder.* There was a picture of a woman there; her name, Tanya L. Jameson. I turned up the volume as the reporter cut to a short bald man – Tanya's lawyer. I quickly googled his name and saw he was a top-notch attorney in Georgia.

Wow, she must be loaded, I thought, *or someone's paying her bills.*

The lawyer's statement confirmed what I already knew: the detectives on Jonathan's case were doing a piss-poor job. Plus, the coroner hasn't released the body yet. Then I remembered Sophia's camera. I'd been so distracted with everything the past couple of days I'd forgot all about it. I scanned the room until I spotted it, high on a shelf where no one would notice it. Now I walked over, grabbed it, and removed the memory card, which I inserted into the card reader. As soon as I plugged it into my computer the pictures started popping up. I was surprised at the clarity of the photos despite the heavy rain.

Looking at the photo of the person on the bike and despite the hoody, I knew it had to be Tanya Jameson, and that she had killed my husband. I glanced at the other photos until I and came to one of the woman in the raincoat. This photo wasn't as clear, but it did capture the strings of red hair plastered on her face. The way she was peering in the car gave me the sense that she knew who was in the car with my husband. *But how? Was she one of his other lovers? Was she Tanya's friend? Had they set him up?*

I logged onto Facebook and typed in Tanya's name. There it was, the same picture on the TV screen. I clicked on her profile, pausing when I saw she worked at Brookes Brothers. I started going through her photos and was relieved there weren't any of Jonathan. I scrolled through more, hoping to find a picture of the redhead, but there was nothing. It was mostly pictures of Tanya's work events, along with a couple of her parents. *How did those women know each other?* Then a thought came to me: if Tanya knew Jonathan from work, maybe that's where she knew this redhead. I typed Brookes Brothers into the search engine and clicked on their website, then the directory. I didn't know where to start so I clicked on the Saint Louis Branch and started scrolling through each name with the photos, after ten minutes of scrolling, I came across a photo of a redhead by the name of Ginger Spence – her title, Administrative Assistant to Tanya L. Jameson.

I pulled up the photo I took and tried to do a side-by-side comparison; I couldn't be certain that this was her, but the resemblance was pretty darn close. This couldn't be a coincidence.

I then googled Ginger Spence and learned that her father was Larry Spence, the owner and CEO of Spence's Construction – net worth one hundred million. He was responsible for designing the new twenty-million-dollar shopping plaza in downtown Saint Louis. *Hmmm...* I thought. *Mr. Spence won't have a problem parting with one of those millions if it means protecting his daughter.*

I picked up the phone and dialed Kevin to ask if he could come over and help me with a couple of projects. Thirty minutes later he was at my house, laptop in hand,

"Mrs. Skagel, how are you holding up?"

"I'm doing okay, thanks." Gesturing for him to follow as I walked into the kitchen. "Are you hungry? I made some soup."

"Thanks," he said as he laid his laptop on the countertop and took a seat in one of the barstools.

I served Kevin a bowl of vegetable soup with sourdough bread. "Would you like something to drink?"

"Water is fine, thank you, ma'am."

"No problem, I appreciate you coming over."

"Yes ma'am, whatever I can do to help."

I was glad he said that. We made chitchat as he ate the soup.

"Wow, that was delicious," he stated as he laid his spoon inside the empty bowl. "Jonathan always raved about your cooking." His face reddening, he looked down. "I am sorry ma'am; I didn't mean to –"

I waved my hand before he could finish. "Don't apologize. It's nice to know that my husband bragged about my cooking at work."

Kevin smiled. I got up, grabbed the empty bowl and placed it in the sink, then turned back to him. "I would like for you to help me with something."

"Yes, ma'am, anything."

"You can refuse if you like and I would prefer for you not to ask any questions about why I would like this to be done."

He looked at me nervously.

"I would like your help in setting up a way for money to be transferred to a bank account, untraced. I would also like to know how to send emails without it being traced back to me."

"Ma'am?"

"Let's just say this is to help secure my children's future, this is all I will tell you."

Without further hesitation Kevin opened his laptop.

"I can easily set up an email that will be untraceable," he said, "But I suggest only keeping it active for a week, no more than two. I can help you erase it after that."

Well, that was easy. I took a seat on the barstool next to Kevin and watched as he pecked away at the keyboard, grateful he didn't need any more convincing.

"As for the untraceable account, it may take a couple of days to set this up, but I can get it done," Kevin stated without looking up from his laptop.

"Wow, you are very smart," I said, and I meant it. I was impressed.

"Yes ma'am, I graduated top of my class at Princeton."

"Well, that's nice to know," I said, then I stood up and walked to the living area. I didn't want to hover over him.

Kevin spent the next hour setting up my untraceable email account and instructing me on how to use it. He would be in touch with me in a couple of days regarding the bank account. I thanked him and gave him five hundred dollars for his trouble. He refused at first, but I told him I knew Jonathan had paid him extra to handle some of his personal affairs and that this was no different. He nodded and took the money. If things went as planned, I would definitely compensate him well for his services.

Three days later, Kevin called asking if he could stop by. When he did he gave me a couple of banking numbers and told me he would help me to retrieve the funds once deposited. I was a nervous wreck but didn't ask any questions. I didn't want to know. I was trusting him with a lot, but what other choice did I have?

When he left, I went back on Facebook and found Tanya and Ginger's email addresses. I never understood why people put their entire life and all their personal information on Facebook, but right now it was making my life easier. I composed two emails, one to Tanya and the other to Ginger.

I kept them short and to the point; I didn't want to give off any clues that could lead back to me. I included pictures of them that day in the park with the words, "I know what you did." Then I demanded that each of them deposit one million dollars to the bank account I provided. My palms were sweaty as I sent the emails. There was no turning back. Now it was a waiting game.

Two days later, there was no reply from either of them. I was getting antsy and had hoped they hadn't gone to the police with my emails. For all I knew the cops could be investigating the bank account right now. All I could do was pray Kevin had been successful in covering my tracks.

~ ~ ~

A couple of months passed. During that time, the coroner had finally released Jonathan's body so we could have a proper burial, and I was getting back into a normal routine with the kids. I would be lying if I said I didn't miss Jonathan. He was my first love, my first everything, and the father of my two amazing kids. No matter what he had done I would always love him for that.

Money had continued to be a worry for me; then one day I received a call from an insurance agent. He informed me of a life insurance policy Jonathan had taken out with Brookes Brothers shortly before his death. I would be receiving a payout after all, and though it wasn't the million dollars I'd hoped for it, along with the policy I had taken out on Jonathan, this would be enough to keep me and the kids comfortable for a while.

As I headed out to run errands one Saturday morning, I received a call from Kevin. He informed me that a transfer in the amount of four hundred and thirty-eight thousand dollars was pending in my account. I was shocked. I had forgotten all about that account; I assumed that Kevin would close it after a couple of weeks. I pulled out my phone and opened the fake email account. There were two messages, both from Ginger.

I clicked on the first one, which read: *Who is this? This isn't me in the photos. How do I know this will be the end of it?* I clicked on the next email, which included a confirmation of the bank transfer, along with the words, *this is all I have right now. I will get you the rest, but it must be in person. Let me know when and where.*

I closed the email, then called Kevin and asked him to delete the email account. This whole blackmailing thing wasn't me and I was a bit ashamed that I had done it. Then again, Ginger was involved with the murder of my husband. I decided to put that money in a special account for the kids to have when they got older. They deserved it.

CHAPTER 23

JONATHAN SKAGEL

I knew who she was as soon as she rushed through the door of the conference room. She was late, but lateness was expected from Ms. Tanya L. Jameson. Everyone at Brookes Brothers knew this. It wasn't a good look for the VP of Finance. I watched as she frantically glanced around the room looking for an empty seat. Lucky for me, there was one at my table. It must have been fate.

She walked over and sat, then started fumbling in her tote bag for something. Finally she pulled out a notepad, then glanced up and noticed that everyone at the table was looking at her. I returned her nervous smile with my flashy one, then held her eye for a moment before looking back toward the stage. During the conference, I could feel the heat of her gaze burning through the back of my neck. Oh, this was going to be easy, "this" being getting close to Tanya to find out what I needed to do to get on Charles Jr.'s good side. I had no problem with Charles Sr.; Charles Jr, on the other hand, was the reason I'd been passed over for Senior Vice President three years in a row. The promotion would have meant a twenty-thousand-dollar increase in salary, along with a hefty annual bonus. Every year he found some bullshit excuse as to why I wasn't ready for the position.

Charles Jr. had hated me from the moment I walked into the interview room eight years ago. I could tell from the condescending look on that smug face of his. Everyone else was pleasant, except him. I didn't care; I knew was winning over the other partners. He'd hadn't stopped me from getting hired at Brookes Brothers, but he sure was making sure I didn't advance there. I was the only director of a branch who wasn't a Senior VP, which made me and my branch look "less than" compared to the others; in fact, I had already lost two of my main employees to other branches because of it. Charles Jr. was keeping my entire branch down and I needed to get to the bottom of this.

One night, while Ginger and I were lying in bed, she told me about her boss Tanya and how Charles Jr was in love with her. Tanya wasn't into him like that, Ginger said; Tanya's love life was basically non-existent. That's when I came up with my plan. At nearly forty, Tanya was surely looking for the right man to sweep her off her feet, and I was just the man to do so. I kept my inquiry about Tanya vague so as not to alarm Ginger. She was fun but I didn't trust her to keep this a secret, especially since I didn't know how far I'd have to go with Tanya to get the information I needed. Sure, Ginger claimed to be this hard shell of a woman with no feelings, but I knew that was a façade. I didn't want her suddenly catching feelings and ruining my plans. I knew I would be playing with danger messing with them both, but I was willing to take that chance.

I had no plans to attend the conference in Charlotte until Ginger suggested visiting at our usual spot in Chicago. She stated her boss would be at a conference so she could take off. I inquired about the conference and the next day asked my assistant to register me and to book my flight. I needed to get close to Tanya, and this was the perfect time to do so.

~ ~ ~

Two months after the conference my relationship with Tanya was going well, but there was one problem: she refused to talk about work. It didn't matter how hard I tried or how sneaky I was, she would just look at me with those big brown eyes, touch my hand, and say, "No work talk." I thought about ending it with her since I wasn't going to find out anything about Charles Jr., but I found myself intrigued by her. I understood Charles Jr.'s fascination with her. There was a reason I didn't go for women like Tanya, successful, beautiful, smart. The flaky ones, like Ginger, were easy; they never held my interest past the bedroom. However, women like my wife and Tanya put a spark in me that was hard to put out. Now I was falling for Tanya, and falling hard.

When I proposed to her, I meant it. I was honestly thinking about leaving my wife for her. In the end, though, I couldn't go through with it. Two years earlier, when my mother passed away, I saw the emptiness in my father's eyes. I remembered the way he used to look at my mother, with love and adoration. I didn't understand it then but I understood it now. He loved her with every muscle in his body. When my mother died, a piece of him died with her. He no longer did the things he loved; he just sat in a chair in my sister's house by a window every day as if he was waiting to die. I noticed the same look of adoration in Sylvia's eyes when she looked at me. There was no way I could do that to her.

I didn't know how to tell Tanya that I couldn't marry her and the reason why, so I just became very distant. I felt this was for the best, that she would just move on quietly, but she didn't. She kept calling, even from different numbers, and texting me. Then suddenly, to my great relief, the calls and the texts stopped. It was over.

A couple of weeks later, I received a call from Charles Jr. requesting detailed documents of all my accounts. This was strange, since he'd never asked for these documents before. Kevin, my assistant, had been out of the office for three weeks visiting his sick mother in Maine. He was the only child and needed to be with her during her surgery and recovery. I had Ruby, the assistant from HR, filling in for Kevin while he was gone. She wasn't good at managing my accounts, but she was good at keeping the phones answered and keeping me informed of what was going on in the office, mostly the gossip.

Needless to say, money had been disappearing from my accounts for almost a month and I had no idea about it. My world started to crash down on me. I'd always been able to come out on top, but lately my luck hadn't been so good. I wasn't focused, and in the past six months I had lost all our savings to my gambling habit. No one knew about it, and I expected it to stay that way. I had been shuffling bills like a chess game and was close to losing everything.

When Charles Jr. asked for documentation I didn't have, I knew I was screwed. After reviewing my accounts, I saw the withdrawals but had no clue who was behind them. It had to be an inside job, though; Brookes Brothers had top-notch firewalls. Who had it out for me? I'd hurt a lot of people in this company, mostly women, so it could be any number of them.

The meeting about the missing money was on Friday. After stressing for two days, I got the breakthrough I needed. When Ginger called I wasn't in the mood to talk to her but I answered anyway. She told me that Ruby had informed her of what was going on. I was pissed at Ruby for spreading my business, but when Ginger stated that she knew who was behind it a sense of peace came over me. Typical Ginger – she wanted to meet in person to deliver this news, so we met at a small coffee shop two hours outside of Saint Louis. She smirked as she informed me that Tanya was behind setting me up. I was stunned, both by the news and at Ginger's pleasure in telling me, but then Ginger told me she knew I'd been seeing Tanya. I told Ginger that I didn't believe her, that Tanya would never do anything so underhanded. She laughed and pulled out bank statements displaying transfers that correlated exactly to the amounts and dates of the withdrawals from my accounts. I reviewed the statements in disbelief. Turned out Tanya had more balls than me; she was willing to risk her career to destroy mine.

"I owe her an apology," I said out loud without thinking.

Ginger glanced up at me in shock. "What? Apologize to her?"

"Yes, she is obviously hurt."

"She is framing you… she is beyond hurt!" Ginger said angrily.

"I know, but maybe she'd explain things to Charles if I apologize to her."

"You sound crazy. Are you planning on leaving your wife for her?" Ginger questioned.

"No!"

"Then your apology won't matter."

"So how am I supposed to get out of this?"

"I have access to this account…"

"How?"

"Don't worry about that."

"So, what are you saying, you're going to put the money back?"

"Hell no! That would be stupid. I'm planning on transferring it to one of my father's offshore accounts."

"What?"

"A deposit that size won't raise any flags since he regularly receives them. I'll withdraw it once it clears and I'll split it with you."

"Split it with me? Ha, what makes you entitled to any of this money? I'm the one being ruined by this."

Ginger smirked. "Okay, how about a forty-sixty split, and that's my final offer. Maybe you can take the money and work on getting yourself a new job…? At least this would alleviate some stress."

If she only knew how deep I was under. Three hundred thousand wouldn't go that far, but it would help.

"Okay, but I don't want to lose my job."

"Fine, then fight for it. I can still do what I do, and no one will know."

"Tanya's been calling me lately. Maybe I can meet up with her and record her confessing. I will bypass Charles Jr. and go straight to his father; he'll have her arrested in a heartbeat."

"Sounds like a plan."

"But I need you there, Ginger."

"Why do I need to be there?"

"In case she denies it; I need a witness on my side."

Ginger shrugged, and I knew she was in it with me.

"Thank you, Ginger."

"Yeah, whatever." Then she stood and walked out of the coffee shop.

For the first time in two days, my headache went away. I had a solution and could get everything I wanted out of this.

~That day in the park~

When Tanya shot me, it literally took the breath out of me. I honestly thought I was dying. Desperately gasping for air, I couldn't imagine what it must feel like to get shot without a bulletproof vest on. I'd bought the vest from this kid off Craigslist because my daughter Sophia needed it for a school play. And, by some miracle, I'd thought about it while planning to set up Tanya. The special thing about this vest was that it was laced with red dye. Once punctured, the red dye would explode, giving the appearance of blood. It was ingenious. I didn't think Tanya would shoot me, but I wanted to be prepared just in case. I'm glad I was.

I was surprised and relieved when Ginger appeared at the passenger door. Had Tanya found me still alive who knows what she would have done. I was still dazed and trying to catch my breath as Ginger peered into the vehicle at me. She wasn't aware of the vest either. I reached out to her, trying to let her know our plan had worked. But instead of grabbing my hand, Ginger just gave me a weird look. At first I thought she was scared for me, and though I felt bad I needed her to snap out of it. I wanted her to call the cops so they could arrest Tanya for this. But Ginger just stared at me and after a couple of minutes she just shut the door. I couldn't believe it; she thought I was dying and instead of helping me she was just going to leave me there.

I unzipped the vest, now covered in red dye, and pulled it off me. I didn't realize how heavy it was. With this thing off me, I was finally able to catch my breath. I reached on the floor of the backseat and retrieved the recorder that I'd placed there when I entered the park. The record button was still pressed. I clicked the stop button and pressed the rewind button. A smile formed on my face when I heard Tanya's voice. *This is what I needed,* I thought. I could give this to the cops and have her arrested for attempted murder.

As I sat listening to the recording, I was startled by a loud thud that hit my car. "Shit!" I said out loud, I hoped that whatever it was didn't make a dent; this was a rental and I couldn't afford to shell out any money for damages. I was already going to have to get this car detailed tomorrow hoping that the dye would come out. I grabbed my jacket off the back seat, put it on and got out of the vehicle to view the damage. The rain had slowed to a light drizzle, so I walked around the car to look for the culprit behind the loud bang. There is was – a large rock lying by one of the tires. *Where the hell did this come from?* I thought as I rubbed my hand over the noticeable small dent on the side of the vehicle. I jumped when I heard a crackling sound, then spun around.

"What the hell are you doing here?" I asked.

CHAPTER 24

CHARLES BROOKES JR.

From the first time I met him, I knew Jonathan Skagel would bring our company down, the company that my father worked so hard to build. Well, there was no way I was going to let that happen. My father couldn't see through him, but I did.

When I found the discrepancy in Jonathan's report, I knew this was my chance to get him fired but I had to build the case against him. I immediately called Todd, the director of our IT department, and asked him to look into it for me. It wasn't long before he traced the transfers from Jonathan's account to Tanya's IP address. I asked Todd to keep watching the accounts and not to tell anyone. He was loyal, so I knew he would do exactly what I asked. I needed to keep Tanya's name out of this for as long as I could. At first, I couldn't figure out why Tanya would be moving money from Jonathan's account and risking her employment at Brookes Brothers, but then I remembered how tense she'd become when I spoke about Jonathan's wife and kids. She was having an affair with him, and it had gone bad – it was the only explanation for why she would be risking her career like this. Todd updated me each time a transfer happened. They started off small then increased. I had to cut it off once it reached four hundred and thirty-eight thousand because my father would kill me if he knew I was just sitting back watching this lover's quarrel happen, putting our company in jeopardy.

I loved Tanya; I'd loved her from the first time she walked into our company as an intern. I admired the way she carried herself, with such poise. My father didn't think she was cut out for this business; he said she was too soft. I had to convince him to offer her a position. I promised him that she would work under me and that if anything happened I would take full responsibility. My father agreed, and Tanya accepted our offer and started working for Brookes Brothers. After I showed her the ropes, she proved my father wrong. He was impressed with her and told me that I had an eye for raw talent. I really only had eyes for Tanya. I was happy that she turned out to be a great asset to the company and that we became great friends. I tried on many occasions to get closer to her but she always pushed me away. She would constantly remind me and everyone around us that she thought of me as the brother she never had. I figured if I showed her how much I cared for her she would eventually see me differently. That's why I lied to her about my place being remodeled. I was tired of playing it safe and needed to show her that I could be the man that she wanted to come home to every night.

~ ~ ~

Firing Jonathan was going to be the best day of my life. He'd been a thorn in my side for eight years and now I was finally going to pluck him out. But when I went to my father to obtain his signature on the termination paperwork, he wouldn't sign it.

"He has a family, Charles," he said, "Besides, what investigation have we done on our end? Has Todd looked into this?" I lied and said no; I wasn't prepared to let my father know how long I'd been aware of this.

"Let's just put him on suspension until we can figure this out."

I left my father's office furious, not at him but at myself. Dad was right; I'd acted too fast on this. I should've investigated more into where the money was going; I should've made my case solid. I walked back to my office and looked at the clock. Thirty minutes until Jonathan was to arrive. I sat there, angrily rephrasing the speech in my mind from, "You're fired" to "You've been suspended."

I heard a light knock on my door; it was Tanya wearing a stunning red dress that was borderline inappropriate for work. She looked damn good, though, and she smelled sweet. I was sure Ginger had told her that Jonathan was coming in and this was why she was in my office. It was evident when she stuttered and made up bogus questions. I wasn't about to have them flaunt their relationship in my face. I looked at the clock again; there were ten minutes until he got there and I needed Tanya out of my office now. I made some excuse about having to make a phone call, but when she opened the door to leave, there was Jonathan, chatting with Renee, my assistant. He acted as if he barely knew Tanya and I could tell that she was hurt. I was angry at him for that.

~That day in the park~

I was out for my normal Saturday morning run, hoping to see Tanya as I usually did. Saturdays were her long runs and if I timed it right I could catch her on the tail end. Most of the time, I would just watch her and run from a safe distance behind. I pulled the watch that her father gave her out of my pocket and looked at the time. She loved this watch, but lately she'd complained at how the shorthand would get stuck so she didn't wear it as much. I had taken the watch to get it fixed for her, but once I had it, I felt closer to her and couldn't part with it.

This Saturday was different. Instead of being on foot, Tanya was riding a bike. Although she wore a black hoody, I knew it was her; I could spot her anywhere. I ran across the street and followed her into the familiar park, keeping a safe distance. My eyes transfixed on her, she didn't even notice me. Following her to a remote part of the park, I saw her place her bike against the tree. I started to call after her but then noticed she was walking towards a parked car. Then I saw him, Jonathan; he got out of the vehicle and walked towards her. She appeared tense as he wrapped his hands around her, but she didn't reject his embrace. I wanted to smack the smug look off his face. When he let her go, she walked over to the passenger side of the car and got in. The rain started and I moved under the pavilion. As Tanya and Jonathan sat in the car, I wondered what they were discussing. Were they in this together? Was Tanya stealing the money for him? I gagged at that thought. My mind was circling with thoughts and ideas.

The sound of a gunshot shook me out of my daze, then I saw Tanya flee from the vehicle. I noticed something drop from her pocket, but she didn't realize it; she just quickly got on her bike and peddled off. I couldn't take my eyes off her. *What did you do...?* I thought was I watched her disappear into the woods.

I noticed someone approaching – a woman in a lime-green raincoat. She walked to the open passenger door of the car, peered in, then slammed the door closed and walked back in the direction she'd come from. I remembered that lime green coat from somewhere but could not recall where... my mind was scrambled. Who was this person? What had I gotten myself involved in? I sat on the bench under the pavilion with my head in my hand, thinking of what I should do. There was no way I could explain why I was at the park and what I'd witnessed without implicating Tanya. That's when I saw movement in the car.

Was Jonathan alive? I squinted to see inside the vehicle. The rain had let up by then and I could see his face; in fact, he appeared to be smiling! What in the hell was going on? I noticed him looking down at something. Was he okay? I was about to call the police but I needed to know how hurt he was before I got myself more involved. I stood up, intending to walk to the vehicle to get a better look and stepped on a large rock. Without thinking, I picked it up and threw it at his vehicle. A minute later, Jonathan stepped out of the vehicle, clearly unhurt. I was even more confused now. I didn't even think about what I was doing; I knew I just needed to confront him.

He heard my approach and spun around. "What the hell are you doing here?"

I continued walking towards him and saw what had dropped from Tanya's jacket. It was the gun. I picked it up and looked at Jonathan. He looked flustered and started walking around to the driver's side door.

"Stop!" I stated, holding the gun up to him.

"Hold up, man, what's going on?"

"You just couldn't let her be, could you?"

"Wow… this is some real Romeo and Juliet bullshit."

I looked to the ground, slightly embarrassed.

"Wait… she doesn't even know that you're here, does she?" Jonathan questioned.

"Shut up."

"Wow, I thought she was lying about you…"

"What do you mean?"

"She knew you were following her around town, appearing in stores she would be at, in restaurants, just to watch her. She told me all about it. We laughed over it after I made love to her one night."

"Shut up! You don't know what you are talking about."

"I didn't believe her because you didn't seem like that type, but seeing you here all disheveled, fighting for her honor, I see this is true. Maybe if you showed this side of you more often, you would have her." Jonathan let out a devilish laugh. "My lawyer is going to have a field day with this…"

Jonathan opened the driver's side door, then peered at me. "You are weak, this is why Tanya has never and won't ever love you! You allow her to walk all over you, everyone in the office sees it and laughs at you."

Jonathan got in the vehicle and begin fumbling with the keys, I couldn't let him get away. I jogged to the passenger side door and got in before he could lock the doors.

I looked into his eyes and saw that smug smile of his. A flicker of a red blinking light caught my eye, I glanced down and saw that he was holding something tight in his hand. It was a recorder; he had recorded everything – Tanya, and now me. *This was a setup,* I thought.

I reached over to take the recorder from him but he had a tight grip on it. With his free hand grabbed my fingers, squeezing them so tight the blood immediately rushed out of them. As I screamed out in pain, Jonathan grabbed my other hand, attempting to get the gun. I panicked and tried to fire a shot towards the window, intending to scare him, but he lunged towards me and the bullet hit him in the chest. He tried to grab my arm but the wetness of my jacket wouldn't allow him to get a firm grip and he slumped back instead; a dark red stain spreading out over his chest. He fought to catch his breath, but no air was coming through. I watched as he gasped for the last time, then his eyes closed. I grabbed the recorder from his now open hand and exited the vehicle, not looking back.

EPILOGUE

VERONICA REDMOND

One year later

"**S**weetie, I forgot an ingredient, I am going to run to the store." Victor leaned down and kissed me on the lips before heading out of the house. Today was our one-year dating anniversary and he was preparing a Caribbean feast for us. I'd thought having a long-distance relationship would be hard, but it wasn't. Most months I either went to D.C. to see him or he came to Georgia – it wasn't ideal, but it worked for us. The job was going well, and I was settling into my new city. Storm hinted every day about retiring again. The more Storm hinted, the more Victor hinted about moving here full-time and taking over for him. It would be a huge change for him career-wise, and it meant a lot to me that he would be willing to consider it.

"I think we make a great team... on and off the force," he would say, and it always brought a smile to my lips, because it was true.

It was a nice evening, and I decided to go outside and sit on the swing until Victor came back. Six months ago, I'd purchased a small house close to the ocean and I loved it. I was about to slip out the door when I saw a dark SUV coming up my driveway. I wasn't expecting any company. With my hand on the gun that lay on the table by the door, I waited as the vehicle pulled to a stop. A white man of medium height got out and started walking my way, a manila envelope in his hand. As he got closer, I recognized who it was. I relaxed my hand and stepped out the door. The man didn't have on an oversized suit this time, nor the timid look on his face I remembered, but a tailor-made suit that made him appear much taller. He also walked with confidence and had a reassuring presence.

"Detective Boatman!" I called out.

"Detective Redmond, I was wondering if I could have a word with you," he stated as he held up the manila envelope.

I glanced at it, then looked up into his eyes.

"Sure, why don't you come in…"

Thank you to my readers: I hope you enjoyed reading this book as much as I enjoyed writing it.

With love,

S.J. Boyce

authorsjboyce@gmail.com

Made in the USA
Coppell, TX
26 January 2023